ONE AND LAST LOVE

And that's the first time I met Vivien . . . I had absolutely no intimation that my life was going to change. Tim Harnforth before that meeting and Tim Harnforth now are almost two different persons. The only love I really had experienced then at its fullest was love for my children. There was a coldness at the heart somewhere. I hadn't ever really loved a woman. I hadn't ever given myself. There'd been a certain amount of affection, but no more. I think that they all knew it. There would be moments with them all when they'd be speaking a different language and there'd be a certain sadness in their voices when they realized I hadn't understood that language . . .

Also by John Braine
in Methuen Paperbacks

LIFE AT THE TOP
THE CRYING GAME
STAY WITH ME TILL MORNING
THE QUEEN OF A DISTANT COUNTRY

JOHN BRAINE

One
and Last Love

METHUEN LONDON LTD

A Methuen Paperback

ONE AND LAST LOVE
ISBN 0 417 07310 0

First published in Great Britain 1981
by Eyre Methuen Ltd

Copyright © 1981 by John Braine

Grateful acknowledgement is made to Faber and Faber Ltd
for permission to reprint lines from *The Libertine*
by Louis MacNeice.

This edition published 1982
by Methuen London Ltd
11 New Fetter Lane, London EC4P 4EE

Reproduced, printed and bound in Great Britain by
Hazell Watson & Viney Ltd, Aylesbury, Bucks

To Geoffrey Strachan, best of editors

'From things that have happened and from things as they exist and from all things that you know and all those you cannot know, you make something through your invention that is not a representation but a whole new thing truer than anything true and alive, and you make it alive, and if you make it well enough, you give it immortality. That is why you write and for no other reason that you know of. But what about all the reasons that no one knows?'

Ernest Hemingway

from *Paris Review*
interviewed by George Plimpton

One

'You're like a boy,' Vivien says to me. 'You're so young, your skin's so smooth...'

'You see me with the eyes of love.' Indeed she does: I never have any doubt about it. Other women have said they loved me, other women have praised my body. I don't think that I really look like a boy, but my body is as she describes it, in better shape than I deserve at the age of fifty-six. It's really an old-fashioned body, an Irish navvy's body, a Regimental Sergeant-Major's body, built for endurance rather than speed. I'm rather fond of it in a detached sort of way: it has broken down from time to time, it isn't one hundred per cent efficient, but somehow or other it always works; and it has begotten four fine children, and given me much more pleasure than pain. It's nothing to boast about, but it's all there – tonsils, appendix, foreskin, the lot. I take reasonable care of it and have never gone in for anything as strenuous as jogging or squash or tennis. I have known middle-aged men die in mid-air leaping the tennis-net, a foolish grin frozen on their faces.

And now my body gives Vivien pleasure. I know that she means what she says, because she always does. I sometimes have the feeling that she wouldn't know how to tell a lie. She's not an idiot: under certain circumstances she'd keep her mouth shut or produce, without any irony in her voice, a reasonably mollifying but essentially noncommittal statement. This is what civilized people do. So what she says outright, I believe. I'm not happy merely because she

9

praises my body but because this faithful companion of fifty-six years also gives her happiness.

These thoughts go through my mind quickly, they are part of our being together. I can always speak my thoughts to her. If we could read each other's minds, we'd still love each other. When she answers me, it's as if there were words beyond her words.

'Of course I see you with the eyes of love. But other women see how attractive you are. My Mr Ajax.' This endearment derives from her childhood in Chatham. Her father was a Lieutenant-Commander, RN, and the Ajax class somehow or other meant to her young and clean-cut masculinity.

I notice for the thousandth, the three thousandth time how pleasant her voice is, on the verge of contralto, strong, distinct, unaffected, easy. 'I saw them at the party last night.'

'There's only one woman for me.'

'That's what you say. I don't altogether trust you.' She tugs my hair gently. 'You have a wild streak.'

'So I may have. But you are the only woman for me.'

We're lying in bed in a flat off Monkman Street, off Shaftesbury Avenue, at four o'clock on a June afternoon. The bed is king-sized, with a white padded headboard and matching white bedside cupboards, with a pink-shaded bedside lamp on each.

'So I may have. But you are the only woman for me.'

Outside, it's a bit too hot – ninety in the shade, not the faintest breeze, and carbon monoxide from millions of exhausts filling up the great chalk bowl of London. There is noise, the greasy smell of onions and hamburgers frying, the sickly smell of popcorn, the smell of the sort of ice-cream that's sold in the streets, a parody of vanilla, and the smell of sweat. And irritation and fatigue, for the heat doesn't really suit London. London likes a snap in the air, London likes the wind and the rain and the mist. Inside the flat it's cool and quiet, the sound of the traffic is as if at a great distance. The quietness is almost physical. Our bodies accommodate themselves perfectly to each other; I feel weightless, released from all physical limitations, yet warm and secure.

We've been coming here every Thursday for nearly four years. Each time it's different, as if for the first time. I watch her undress with mounting excitement, sometimes I can't wait until she's entirely naked but take her in her bra and slip, standing up or kneeling by the bed. I never tire of looking at her, I love every part of her. Her breasts are full but still firm, her legs long. I never think of her age, which is forty-eight. It doesn't matter. There's a hysterectomy scar half-hidden in the black pubic hair. I have great tenderness for that scar and the faint stretch marks on the belly. I have seen a great many naked women, most of them much younger than me. But always after two or three months, sometimes only weeks, there'd be the desire to move on, to see what other women looked like under their clothes. And there wouldn't be any tenderness.

I'm not a boor. There have always been the pretty words, at least the show of affection. But nevertheless with every woman until Vivien what has mattered has been the act itself. I've grown adept at gift-wrapping it. With Vivien what matters is all that surrounds the act. There is no calculation. We don't look at our watches. When we go to bed after a simple lunch – generally salt beef pita sandwiches and tea – we go after a leisured talk. We make love at least once, sometimes twice or thrice. We have a bath together, we have another light meal, we go to the cinema or a theatre or a party, or see friends, or we stay in the flat longer and eat a more elaborate meal.

I'm breaking one of my sacred rules now, I'm telling you and not showing you. I'm telling you the story of a happy love and I'm telling you it now. (I say that I'm telling you it now, but I shan't try to give a date to now. Now is when you read it.) I start in the flat off Monkman Street because it's at the centre of our relationship. And it's in London. This is

11

mostly a London story. So there's space in it, there's all kinds of possibilities. We may have lost our Empire but this is still the capital and this is where all the action is.

My story is about a love affair which started four years ago when I, Tim Harnforth, was fifty-two, and she, Vivien Canvey, was forty-four. I put that down to get things straight. The action of the story is continuing in the flat, the flow of life goes on. It is now, it's in the present tense but, as I pointed out, it can't be dated. After the first act of love we have been lying in each other's arms.

I live this now. I'm in the flat at Monkman Street now. I'm kissing Vivien now. I don't worry. I set myself no targets. Phrases like *Can I do it again so soon?* or *Does she expect it of me?* are never within distance of my mind.

'You're like a bull,' she says delightedly, her hand going down, caressing.

'Only for you.' Her hand is very gentle, but I catch my breath.

'I wouldn't want you ever not to feel – free. But I'd be off, you know. I wouldn't make a fuss, but I'd be away.'

'Slowly. Very slowly. Now be still.' My hand is searching gently. 'There won't ever be anyone else. It's like the song – "And when he thinks he's past love, he meets his one and last love –"'

We are in the flat now as you read this. Of course we're now also in the world of buff envelopes from the Inland Revenue and nasty letters from the bank and increased school fees and having root canals drained and a bill at the end of it which makes one wonder whether one's parents weren't after all wisest to get rid of all their teeth early. Vivien and I are luckier than most. We would have been even if we'd never met each other, but we, much against our will, have to spend time in this drab world. Who doesn't? I can't express what I mean immediately, but I will later. Let's call it the implacable drabness of things, the feeling that there's no taste or colour, that one pays out more and more and gets less and less. This world will appear briefly in my story by way of contrast. I mention it now because I want to play fair with you. I also want to make it plain that I'm in the same boat as you. But the place I'm in now is the flat in Monkman Street.

And Vivien is over me and I now am a city and this is festival day. The tenderness is with us both, we are two people, two individuals. Love is filling the room. I look at her face, so smooth, so unlined, so rapt. I'm in another dimension. I have my identity yet I've lost it and have been glad to lose it, to have lost it in hers.

And then again we lie still. And there is no sadness and no satiety. We affirm our love with simple words and are silent not because we have nothing to say but because we don't need to say anything. The heavy red velvet curtains on the two big windows are drawn, but there is plenty of light. Somehow in the flat all the light that's going is caught. It's as if it held the light, like a miser cherishing gold coins. And yet it isn't a suntrap; the building was put up in 1905, the windows are large openings to let in light and air. There's never been a better period than the Edwardian for dwelling-places, because the materials and workmanship were superb and so was the design. An Edwardian dwelling-place is always just that: designed not primarily as a projection of one's status or an expression of one's fantasy, but to be lived in, lived in happily. And I think this now, lying beside Vivien. It doesn't bother me whether I'm profound or even original, I like using my brain. During the four years I've known her, I've become more and more alive.

I'm lying in bed with Vivien, enjoying quietly looking at the warm tone of her skin, creamy rather than sallow, and her black hair and hazel eyes and strongly marked eyebrows. It's a Regency face with a high-bridged nose; it's a shade imperious but never cold, always responsive, always alive. It's never frightened. I think it was Max Eastman who said of the women of the 1917 Russian Revolution that they had the faces of those who would walk up to the cannon mouth. Vivien would walk up to the cannon mouth. That I know as a fact. No, she's not a revolutionary: no, she's not violent: no, she hasn't rescued anyone from drowning or fire. But it's like the story of Nelson as a child. When he was found waiting patiently alone for help, his grandmother wondered that fear and hunger had not driven him away from the spot where he was waiting. 'Fear?' Nelson asked. 'What is fear? I never saw it.' Vivien has never seen fear. I can see that now just as I can see that her face is the face of a mature woman. It doesn't pretend to be the face of a young woman. It hasn't been lifted, the smooth skin sits easily on the bones. It isn't stretched, it isn't fragile, it would take the wind and the rain in its stride. Her expressions mirror her feelings; they occur, they're not arranged with an eye to their effect. Her face is a face and not a mask she shelters behind. There are scarcely any lines except at the corners of the eyes. I wouldn't care how many lines there were. I wouldn't care if she looked older than she was. I don't care, come to that, how old she is. I wonder now – quietly, lazily – why looking at her face induces within me so much content-ment. Her eyes now are half-closed. We are lying face to face. My right arm is on the pillow above our heads, lightly touching hers. We are breathing evenly.

The room is lofty for its size. It's large enough comfort-ably to accommodate the king-size bed, the large mahogany wardrobe, two mahogany bedside tables, and a mahogany dressing-table. The bed is modern, the rest of the furniture was, I think, bought new when the first tenant moved in. It's all solid, but not heavy, not over-decorated. There's a small oak bookcase too full of paperbacks, mostly thrillers. On the dressing-table there are two matching silver-backed men's hair-brushes, a bottle of Crabtree and Evelyn's honey water, a bottle of Flor Tuberose bath oil, a tablet of Crabtree and Evelyn's wild thyme soap, a large box of Tweed talc, and a green and gold Limoges box in the shape of a book, which contains hairpins and safety pins. The fitted carpet is a dark red Axminster with a gold and blue floral pattern and it's of a heavier quality than is usual in a bedroom. The wallpaper is pale blue with dark red and off-white and dark green stripes. Strictly speaking it doesn't match, it quarrels with the carpet, and the curtains, and everything else, but I don't care. I like the room as it is, I want nothing to change.

When I was growing up I longed for change. Before the War everything was made to last. One didn't replace things when they gave trouble, one patched them up and carried on. Jobs, when one could get them, were for life. Old buildings were torn down, new buildings put up, but soon it was as if the new buildings had always been there. Nobody planned this – the councillors and bureaucrats and developers in those days didn't in the least care about what buildings looked like. As long as they were suitable for their purpose and didn't actually fall down, they were quite happy. Nothing really changed; I found it so oppressive at the age of fifteen that I was very happy when war was declared. And even then the changes were expected changes: the country had been to war before.

But now everything's changing day by day and the new buildings are not only totally hideous, designed for some other planet and some other species, but they keep falling down. All I want is for everything to stay the same. This room hasn't changed since I first came to an arrangement some six years ago to have use of the flat. Raymond Brove, the tenant, lives mostly in Laurel Canyon, Los Angeles. Vivien and I owe him a great deal. This flat is our real home. Here we shut out the world. No one knows the address or phone number. It's our hideaway: Raymond's too, but very rarely. I suspect that he's not the tenant himself, that it's a company flat; Raymond would never be such a peasant – his favourite, if out-dated, term of opprobrium – as actually to sign a lease himself and pay out real money.

One doesn't feel his presence in the flat. But there are in the bedroom half a dozen framed colour stills from films which he has directed: they all feature naked young women

15

with impossibly large and firm breasts and impossibly flat bellies, and naked young men with very broad shoulders, lean flanks and long legs. Raymond's films – so far – aren't exactly pornographic. They're not exactly art either.

I believe that the flats were built ostensibly as *pieds-à-terre* for gentlemen up from the country on business. They were actually love-nests. Rich men kept their mistresses there. (Perhaps St John's Wood was becoming too popular.) Most of the mistresses, understandably in view of the situation of the flats, are supposed to have been actresses, but I have the notion that they were simply expensive whores. There's no denying that the place has atmosphere, that, very unostentatiously, it's opulent, that in a very low voice, correctly but effortlessly modulated, it's raffish: if you're the right kind of person, the voice is saying, do exactly as you please. One doesn't see children here, one doesn't see many young people here, one doesn't see many people here. And those one sees – very briefly in the lift or scurrying along the passage – seem respectable enough. The atmosphere remains: Eros in a top hat and tails.

Again these thoughts are part of the moment I'm living in; Vivien and I are absolutely tranquil, warm but not too warm, relaxed, almost floating, yet rejoicing in each other's palpable physical presence, with no questions, no doubts, no regrets, no fears, no guilts. And I don't feel shame at my nakedness. With all the women in my life before, there's always been a time when, if only for a split second, there was a feeling of shame, even with my two wives. This absolute contentment which we have now built up slowly over the years, has come upon us almost without our knowing it. It couldn't have been expected immediately, we had slowly to find our way towards each other.

And we are there. I'm still astounded by it. I'll never cease to be grateful for it. And now for a while the thinking is over. And the worries – Simon, Penelope, Vanessa, Val, the overdraft, the rewrites on the TV script I'm working on, the recurrent pain in my stomach – which even now try to

16

creep into my mind, all vanish. They are not there. I'm drifting off to sleep, I'm letting go. I'm absolutely safe, I care about nothing any more except Vivien's proximity. *And sleep come down like death above The fever and the peace of love* – but not quite like death. There is a surging, a gliding, Vivien's arms around me, and then I'm in the dream, the best dream I've ever had.

I'm in a field, a big field with drystone walls, high up in Casterley on the verge of the moors. It's northern, the sky is grey, the drystone walls are grey, the grass is short. The moors are above, there are no walls there, they roll away into the distance. The drystone walls are built without mortar – mostly flat stones laid upon each other. They stay up and they're beautiful, because the stone has to be local, it's what is lying around. I don't know whether anyone builds them any more, but 'build' is the wrong word. It's as if the stones were coaxed into place, persuaded that being part of a wall was what they wanted to be. This is Yorkshire, where I haven't lived these twenty-five years.

Yorkshire is part of me, Yorkshire is the place I visit again and again in my dreams, but almost never happily. Why is this so, for I love Yorkshire? But in the Yorkshire of my dreams I'm always lost. Everything has changed and there is always danger and fear and bad weather, tigers and earth tremors, guns and knives and gallows. But this dream is different. It isn't bad weather. It's grey, it's cool, there's rain in the wind, but this one expects in Yorkshire. I enjoy it because I enjoy weather – real weather, weather with variety. And in the dream it's Yorkshire weather, weather one can put up with, not actually raining yet, and I'm grooming a bull, a fine bull, a deep red-brown. I'm brushing him with a soft brush, his coat is glistening, he stands perfectly docile. I reach his legs and he lifts each one up in turn to make it easier for me. There is absolutely no fear. I'm not taming him, I'm not subduing him, I love him and he loves me. He's every inch a bull, with great powerful shoulders tapering to lean flanks. He knows that he's a bull

17

and he's proud of being a bull.

There's a white stone building nearby. The white is off-white, stained dark green with lichen. It's weathered, the tone varies, it's an old building, a companion of the landscape. The windows are small and deep-set, the floors will be stone and the furniture oak. I know that, but I know nothing of the people who live there. They may well know me better. I may well be part of their dream. The bull belongs there; how and in what part of it doesn't matter. I pat the bull on the shoulders and he follows me like a dog. Near the building are about a dozen ponies standing quite still with little girls on their backs, the little girls' voices rising high and happy. No one is frightened of the bull. There's no fear in my dream. I'm not lost. No one is lost in this dream.

I awake smoothly; this is the whole dream, it is complete and perfect. Dreams often break off at the moment of unbearable terror or unbearable ecstasy. This is like a poem. I resolve to keep it. I once faithfully recorded every dream for a month – it must be done immediately one awakens – but I gave it up because in the end the dreams seemed to be too literary, too contrived.

I let Vivien sleep, though I want to tell her about the dream. There is always something I want to tell her about, and she is always interested. But I'm content to enjoy the aftertaste of the dream; I'm lucky to have had it. She has moved away from me in her sleep. She always sleeps on her right side with her mouth closed. I can just see her face. I've seen the sleeping faces of many women; too many, she would say. Some women's faces sag: hers merely composes itself.

I light a cigarette. I'm of the cigarette generation just as I'm of the movie generation. It's five-thirty. I fix the dream firmly. I'm sorry to have to look at my watch but I'm aware that soon we'll have to start planning for the evening. There never is enough time. When I'm with Vivien time always goes with frightening rapidity. It always has done from the first day we met. I keep on being astounded by it. Life is heightened, I'm living as I ought to live. All of me responds, and there is no division between mind and body.

Now Vivien opens her eyes and smiles at me. 'What time is it, darling?'

'A quarter to six.' I kiss her forehead. 'I've had a dream. A marvellous dream . . .'

I tell her about it: it's all absolutely clear in my mind now, but telling her will help me to fix it. She listens intently and she believes me; she knows that it's the whole dream, that I haven't tidied it up.

'What does it mean, do you think?'

'I don't know. I have to think about it. I'm pleased about it, though. He really was a beautiful bull.'

'Was he a brave bull?'

'I expect he was. But he wasn't one of those fighting bulls. Don't like bullfights, anyway. Bloody degenerate. Just what you'd expect from bloody foreigners.'

'Oh God, you're an old reactionary! You never cease to shock poor old Neil.'

'I know. I bet I shock the whole of Hampstead. Neil must get a lot of sympathy.' Neil is Vivien's husband.

We don't make conversation but at moments like this we lazily and amiably push words between each other, our essential selves sauntering arm-in-arm together. There is a silence now but it isn't awkward.

'The dream does mean something,' I say at last. 'All dreams do. They're messages from deep down. Not Freudian, though.' And now I'm trying to find symbols, establish a pattern, I'm using the front part of my brain. I'm becoming nervous, I'm becoming worried, I'm expecting the bull and the ponies and the little girls and the moors and the old stone buildings and the drystone walls to stop being themselves. I'm aware of this, I'm aware that I'm going wrong, but still I can't help myself. 'Oh Christ,' I say, almost in a whisper, 'there is a meaning'

Vivien puts her hand on mine. 'Shush. Leave it, let it go.

You've got a good brain. The circuits are a bit overloaded, that's all. The meaning will trot up to you in its own good time.'

'You're right. It's just that I get so damned tired. There's so much to do. I sit down in the morning to start the day's work, and then I look at my watch and it's over. The day's going now – '

She kisses me on the mouth. 'Darling, the day's here now. This is the moment we're in. We're so lucky. How many people can take a day off in the working week to make love?'

'I'd rather we had every day together. At the end of the day where do we go?'

'It's no use, pet. You want to go home.'

'To Val? I wouldn't care if I never saw her again.'

'You would care if you never saw the children. You know what it did to you not seeing Kevin.'

'Yes. That wasn't my fault.' I find myself growing angry, not with Vivien and not with my son Kevin, a lecturer in the social sciences at a provincial university now involved in what he imagines to be revolutionary politics.

I hardly know with whom I'm angry. Thinking about my present wife, thinking about my first wife, I feel only bewilderment. Thinking about Neil, Vivien's husband, I feel only bewilderment. And then it turns to anger. 'You could have got a divorce five years ago. But you couldn't leave the children.'

'Yes.' I think of Kevin again. He's taller than me, he's lean and moves quickly, he has eyes like his mother's, a deeper blue than mine, almost startling. He has fair hair like his mother – why do I always marry blondes? – and it's long but not too long. He'd be accepted either in a board-room or at a demo. And his clothes are expensive, casual. He's a good-looking young man and he keeps himself fit without being a fanatic about it. Yes, he's fulfilled. He's an instrument of the revolution, 'Clean, bright and slightly oiled', the way the Army likes its guns to be. But now I remember my last visit to him. We were having a nightcap at about half-past eleven in the living area of his cosy bachelor pad on campus, which he has at a peppercorn rent. It's small, but big enough, clean, quite tidy, the colours light, with a lot of books. He's been there two years. There is more to it than that. There always is.

Kevin and I have been chatting quite amiably about the talk I've given at the Union, and about the University. There are four empty glasses on the big beechwood coffee table: our guests have gone. Kevin is quite animated, but not at all disturbed. He's just a young professional man grumbling, letting off steam. I'm quite interested, but I don't really care: I have a notion that the University will somehow stagger on and that my revolutionary son will keep on climbing up the academic ladder. I excuse myself and go into the bathroom. I return to the living area. Kevin doesn't notice that I return. He's sitting very still in his armchair – it's big, in fawn leather and steel, and rather brutal: I know that it's comfortable because I've been sitting in its twin, but in a curious way it forces comfort upon one, as a certain kind of host presses a drink upon one. Kevin's drink – a stiff whisky on the rocks – is on the table. It doesn't exist for him. The room doesn't exist. I don't exist. I stand there and look at him. No, he isn't about to break down. He's not on drugs. He's not drunk. He isn't particularly tired. He isn't about to cry. But this, for a few seconds, is Kevin the human being.

Kevin the revolutionary is a gun – or is trying to be. Kevin the social sciences lecturer is a sound cassette, a set of graphs, a sheaf of typescript, a pile of annotated textbooks. But what I see now is a human being who has been deserted. There's loss in his face, there's desolation.

I didn't leave my first wife; she left me and took Kevin with her. And her new husband provided her with a four-bedroomed two-bathroomed house near Harrogate and an au pair and a little car of her very own. But Kevin feels that I left him. And that's what is in his face. No words of mine can change what he feels. In a different country now, or at a different time in this country, a hug and a kiss and unfeigned tears would be the answer. Being in England now, being in a country where our natural responses are still poisoned by nineteenth-century stoicism, I can only smile at him and say something pleasant but noncommittal and see his mask take over. It's a splendid mask, the best. I can't tell the mask that when my other children are growing up I shall always be there. It won't help him.

I can't tell him. I can tell Vivien. There is nothing that I can't tell her because this is what love means. There has been, after I've said yes, this picture of Kevin. Then a second's pause. During that second there is no time. We don't do it consciously, it can't be done consciously, but Vivien and I have come to an agreement with time. It's a gentleman's agreement, quite informal. There's no boredom: time doesn't touch the ground, we look at the hands of a clock and it has no message for us, any more than it would have for a baby or a primeval savage. But a second can contain for us as much as we want, time expands for us.

'I wouldn't leave the children. I can't leave the children. They're the one thing that keeps me with her.'

'I wouldn't want you to leave them. You wouldn't have a happy moment.'

'Yes, yes. Still – sometimes I feel all boxed in. I never seem to do what I want to do. Other people do. They seem to get by.'

She smiles. 'Do we care? It's all outside, isn't it? It can't touch us here. I love this place.' She moves her hand down my body and looks at me speculatively. 'Are you rested now?'

'I'd like some tea.'

'Really?' Her hand busies itself, but not urgently. 'So would I. You promised last week that you'd make it today.'

'Vivien make it. Vivien be nice to me. I'm too comfortable to move.'

'Male chauvinist pig.' Her hand stops but stays where it is.

'No, darling. I'm all for equality. I don't consort with my inferiors.'

'A cunning male chauvinist pig. The worst kind.' She puts on the orange silk dressing-gown at the foot of the bed. 'I spoil you. Everyone spoils you. Even Val in her way.'

'I'm worth it. I make you happy.'

She kisses me. 'Oh yes. You do make me happy. It's a very *solid* happiness. Very tranquil. Not that you are tranquil really. You're wild.'

'It's the Mick in me. That's the wild one, the roaring boy. The other's sensible. Down-to-earth. That's the Englishman. You've got two for the price of one.'

'I love them both.'

Kevin returns to my mind and I think again of what I should have done. Words come into my mind and I share them with Vivien. '*Ruffle the perfect manners of the frozen heart And once again compel it to be awkward and alive . . .*'

'That's beautiful. Who is it?'

'Auden. *Spain* – I think he disowned it later.'

She repeated the words, giving them full value, keeping the beat, the wonderful, muscular surge. And it's like the first time I read Auden, back in Casterley Public Library, it's all absolutely fresh. 'You're really stirring me up,' I say gratefully. 'Oh God, if only I could talk more with you! Then I could sort things out. Do you know something? All my life I've been going to sort things out when I had time to spare. I'd like a year now. And I'd tidy up my office and sort out all my books and papers and just sit down and think. And we'd really explore London. And we'd go to all the galleries and museums, we'd see everything worth seeing. And we'd travel. Out of season, that's the only way. We'd have a quiet time, and we'd always be cheerful.'

'You *are* cheerful. You're the most cheerful man I've ever met. Unlike some. Not that he makes any waves these days. We don't talk much.'

'Not like you and me. We never seem to stop.'

She leaves the bed in one graceful movement. 'Except for

tea.' She leaves the room.

I reflect that now it's as it was when I was younger. I have my sense of wonder back, I even have a sort of innocence. I'm starting again. And I know. more, I haven't become blasé but I've calmed down: it's unlikely – though not impossible – that I'll make too big a fool of myself. I lie back in bed now, quite happy, but at the same time missing Vivien. I always miss her when she goes out of the room. I'm honestly not possessive, but we have only this afternoon and evening once a week, four phone calls a week, the odd evening or lunch, the odd day out of London. It's more than most couples get who love as we do. *Who love as we do*: Arletty's phrase from *Les Enfants Du Paradis*, a film which has been part of me ever since I first saw it in Yorkshire in 1946. Those who love as we do want every possible moment together. We aren't greedy, we don't exclude the world. We can't live just for each other. We'd be in a cage then. That's the true *folie à deux*.

More than once women have tried to drag me in that direction. They've constricted me more and more, have tried to push out of my life everyone else.

With Vivien more people have been brought in my life, it hasn't been a question of being caught up in a frenetic social whirl, of seeking new faces desperately, but of reaching out and growing. We welcome new people into our lives, they give to us and we give to them, we make friends. Outside of this flat we're in the mainstream and we want people around us, all kinds of people, delighting in their variety. Here it's only the two of us and it's company enough. And I miss her when she goes out of the room. I like her to be always there, she needn't even speak.

It's an astonishing feeling at the age of fifty-six, acknowledging at last that with every woman until her I've been relieved when they've been absent for a while, that I've been deliberately switching on the charm and a show of affection as recompense for sex and have needed a little time to be myself and to recharge the batteries.

24

I know all the tricks. I'm not a superstud, nor did I ever want to be. But I can't deny that I've always been able to get women easily and that when I was younger it gratified my vanity that I should be able to do so. Now vanity doesn't enter into it. There was a change in my middle forties, a bad patch when I wondered, as someone once said, not so much whether I could do it as whether I wanted to do it. That's all over. And what also is all over is the ridiculous notion that once into middle age it's not really proper to have sex. One's supposed to be past it. And just before I met Vivien there were, in fact, moments when the notion of contracting out had its attractions. Something in me was being eroded. It isn't now. I'm not immune to age or sickness, but while this love lasts my face will never empty totally of sparkle and zest, never become without any sort of alertness. That's what happens to the face when we've let Eros go. We stop fighting, we start acquiescing, we're no longer ready for adventure, for a frisk in the small hours, we become predictable. I'm not ever going to be predictable. I'll always be out of step and proud of it.

I think about this hazily while Vivien's in the kitchen. I also think, quite contentedly, that she's the last one. If she'd been someone else she wouldn't have been the last one. That used to be wearying too. My head is full of pieces of poetry. Lately, they've been coming back more and more often.

> Long fingers over the gunwhale, hair in a hair-net,
> Furs in January, cartwheel hats in May,
> And after the event the wish to be alone –
> Angels, goddesses, bitches, all have edged away:
> O leave me easy, leave me alone . . .

That's it: MacNeice knew. It's not so much the wish to be alone, though, as having gone over the top yet again, of once again having won, of having come through once again unscathed, but knowing that there'll be another battle.

That's how it was. It wasn't grown-up. It wasn't good enough. Somehow it had become a question of power and of ownership. And that was never really for me. I can perceive the attractions of political power and I'm not so high-minded that I can't enjoy ownership – I enjoy at this very moment the solidity of my gold Rolex Oyster and my gold identity bracelet. Portable property is a great consolation. But I don't want power to enter into my personal relationships and I don't want to own any human being.

I think about this whilst Vivien is in the kitchen. And I look at the stills on the wall now: they are notes of physical events, they are important. The one on the far wall shows two naked girls, one dark, one fair, the dark girl looking down on the fair girl with a rather greedy expression, the fair girl looking rather resigned. The film was made in the early seventies when pubic hair could be shown. But not yet the open crotch. The blonde's legs are open wide, but because of the angle from which it's shot, one doesn't see what the brunette is very obviously pleased to see. Nearby there's a naked young man and another naked woman, older than the couple on the mattress, with a carefully made-up face and sunglasses and a gold bracelet and a gold chain and cross round her neck and a thick gold wedding-ring and a diamond engagement ring. She has upswept lacquered ash-blonde hair and looks much more naked than the two younger women. She does actually begin to interest me.

What she is interested in, I think, is the half-full glasses at the little table away to the left. The young man – smooth tan, carefully tousled hair, – is on the face of it well able to be to be actively interested in the woman he's talking to with a flash of capped teeth – but I know that he isn't. I've met his type. He's interested in himself and keeping up his tan and acquiring not only money in the bank but certain specific material objects.

I never saw the film: it wasn't released in the UK. I did meet the blonde girl, a rather spirited German who said to me of the young man, 'He iss all day nekked in bed wiz me and he does not have the decency to have an erection!' She died last February in New York of a heroin overdose. She was twenty-eight. There hadn't been many films; she'd never been a star. But she had been there, she'd registered her presence. I met her at a party at the Dorchester: I'm not quite sure but it must have been before the stills that I'm looking at now were shot. She was wearing a skimpy red dress and not much else; her companion was an old, obese and rather disgusting film producer who pawed her buttocks in an abstracted way from time to time. I had a feeling that what was happening between them wasn't what would make any girl happy. Lise was a nice girl. She had humour in her face too.

'Tea, and Mrs Kippax's Fairy Drops.' Vivien says, putting the tray down on the bedside table and sitting down on the bed. She manages somehow to shift everything from the bedside table to the tray without any fuss. 'Why do you look so sad?'

I nod at the stills. 'I was remembering Lise. The blonde girl. I told you about her.'

She pours the tea. 'Yes. Poor girl. You *said* you didn't go to bed with her. Did you?'

I drink some tea. It's almost as good as a really dry martini, a sudden euphoric glow in my stomach. 'No, I told you, I got on a treat with her – she'd read my books – but her sugar daddy gave me a dirty look.'

'Were you scared?'

'Too true I was. There were two of his underlings nearby. About six foot four. Quite smooth and young and collegiate. But tough. I don't know whether the sugar daddy was doing anything with Lise, but he didn't want anyone else to. Christ, she was a nice girl. I ran into her a couple of times after that. She liked my books, she really did . . . The worst of it is that I'm more and more upset by that sort of thing. One doesn't get tougher. One keeps on losing layers of skin.'

'You'll survive,' she says affectionately. 'You're indestructible.'

'I wish I could be sure of that. It's a horrible world.'

'I'm glad you're not in politics any more.'

'Heard all about the troubles when I was a kid. All about the Black-and-Tans and the gallant Irish rebels. Actually I was rather on the side of the Black-and-Tans. Sheer cussedness.' I begin to eat a biscuit: I have a sense of infinite leisure.

'You were always on the box once. Or on the radio. Quarrelling like mad with everyone. That was before I met you. I loved your books – but, my God, how you shocked me!'

'Don't I shock you any more? Have I corrupted you?'

She giggles. 'I'm not so sure that you haven't.'

'I won't change you, darling. You'll always be a bit starry-eyed in the nicest possible way.' I stroke her hair. 'I don't want to change you. I don't give a damn about politics any more. I'm too tired.'

'Tired?' Has Val been acting up?'

'No. She's very subdued these days. It's as if she knows I always have someone to go to. It's not as it was before. The others didn't mean anything. Because I'd move on to others. But you're the last one.'

'Don't be so sad.' She shifts her position slightly; the dressing-gown falls away from her legs. 'Are you really very tired?'

I find myself breathing very quickly. 'Not when I'm with you.'

She takes off her dressing-gown. Looking down at the gentle curve of her belly she grimaces. 'I'm a fat middle-aged lady.'

'You're perfect.' I want to say that I don't give a damn about anyone else's standards, that though I do care about her body because it's her body, I don't care any more that there are younger firmer women's bodies available. Any more than I care that there are other women available who are no doubt better writers with more penetrating and more subtle intelligences. I did care about this once, I always felt sooner or later that I could have got something better. I was always in competition. I've outgrown all that now. I want Vivien, the person. I'm not frightened any more of what age will do to us: I accept it all, and we will one day listen to the sea together. She climbs in beside me and I say none of this but it's as if I'd said it. There is this closeness and tenderness and tranquillity and also, let there be no mistake about it, there is the fact that we are a naked man and a naked woman in bed together, and to see and touch one another is absolutely and incandescently superb.

We're not measuring time now; her hand travels over my belly. 'Oh, you're not tired. You're really not. What would you like? You can have anything you want.'

'It might be something very shocking. You might spring off the bed, get dressed, and storm out of the flat...'

'You couldn't shock me.' Her hand is busy, but very gently. 'I know what you want.'

Yes, she knows what I want almost before I know. And so this afternoon this is the pattern. It's never a prescribed pattern, though almost always we have what we call the entrée at least once. I suppose that we've read all the books but we don't take any notice of any of them. We do not take, we give. And – this is an essential and urgent message – we make love to each other as the people we are and not as bodies. We always know who we are, Vivien and I. As her dark head moves rhythmically, as I feel her lips and tongue, it *matters*, it is memorable and sacred, it is an expression of love. And when the culmination arrives it isn't a spasm, a spilling, but a long flight like a ski-jump, a smooth and perfect landing and gentle falling gently stopped.

'*My mother wore a yellow dress, Gently, gently, gentleness.*' I speak the words to Vivien now very softly. They have to be spoken softly.

'That's beautiful.' She smiles at me.

'It can't be taken away from me. But I can share it.'

'You used not to talk so much about sharing when first we met.'

'No. But I've grown since then.'

Two

My great-grandfather, Thaddeus Cloneen, came to Wetherford in Yorkshire at some time in the 1850s. Wetherford was then no mean city. It wasn't beautiful and it had some hellish slums, but it had real character. It was built by human beings. They were pretty horrible – as my mother used to say, they'd steal the pennies off a dead man's eyes and cut up his shroud for handkerchiefs. (The pennies she meant were the old pennies, big and heavy.) But they were human beings. Wetherford was tough and money-mad and didn't go out of its way to welcome any newcomers: but if you were tough – and lucky – there'd be some sort of job and some sort of shelter available. Put it this way: there were a lot of corners to hide in.

Thaddeus, my grandmother Cloneen said, was 'a grand big man, six foot in his socks and built like the side of a house'. I can hear her now; she was the first in her family to be born in England and didn't have the brogue but had an Irish turn of speech: 'Ah, he was a fine-looking man with black hair and a great black beard. Without a word of a lie he looked like an Old Testament prophet. And he was the rottenest old hell-devil that ever drew breath.' He was in fact a horse-dealer, got roaring drunk every day of his life, and lived hale and healthy until the age of eighty, dying after a short illness which gave him time enough to receive the Last Sacraments and, indeed, to leave the world in an odour of sanctity.

Most of the immigrants from Ireland to Wetherford were

driven there by poverty. Thaddeus was actually thrown out of Ireland by his family because he drank too much and was a hell-raiser generally. My God, imagine! To be thrown out of Ireland for drinking too much! I'm rather proud of this. He came to Whitegate, the Irish quarter of Wetherford, and set up open house with the £100 until it was all spent. I don't know what the equivalent of £100 would be today — £5,000 would be near it at the moment I'm writing these words. As long as the money lasted anyone who came to his house could have their bellyful of beef and bread and beer.

All this matters. All this is part of me. But it's another story there isn't time to tell. Not that I'm panicking, but time is running short. So I'll tell only the story of Tim and Vivien. And I'll tell it straight.

I did in fact originally intend to have what is termed a good strong plot. The hero was to have received a death sentence from a Harley Street specialist at the beginning. The specialist, a tall man with a dry skin and a cadaverous face, was to have shuffled through X-ray plates absently. The consulting-room would have been lofty but constricted with heavy and shabby furniture and engravings of English cathedrals. The specialist would have had an Edinburgh accent, real cut-glass; there would have been more than a hint of disdain in his manner. The trouble would have been in the brain. There would have been for a long time headaches; bouts of dizziness; bouts of amnesia; pains in the chest which the hero described to himself as heartburn; deep and savage tingling of the legs; strange faces and strange patterns forcing their way into his consciousness even when his eyes were closed; and, more and more smotheringly — a huge dirty grey blanket over the head and hard sweaty hands gripping his arms, hustling him away — depression, *cafard*, *angst*. My hero would have described all this at a previous meeting and would have described it accurately. There would have been more — something perhaps small but humiliating: minor incontinences of the bladder, irrational impulses only just held off by fierce effort of will, like an impulse to pee in a crowded street in broad daylight, like an impulse to throw oneself out of the bedroom window. At this meeting there'd be the X-ray plates and the full medical report. The specialist would have a sheaf of notes, written in a small crabbed hand.

There would have been a certain dry relish in the specialist's voice, he would have seemed rather pleased with himself. He would have painted a vivid but coherent and clear clinical picture, and have been proud of his ability to do so. He would have tried to conceal this and in the process his cut-glass accent would have become even more refined.

'The prognosis, I'm afraid, is not exactly a comfortable one. I've given a good deal of thought to your case, and of course you're free to seek a second opinion – '

His tone would have indicated that there wouldn't be much point in doing so. 'Perhaps if you'd come to me earlier –' and he would have stopped himself from reproving my hero, being mindful of the fact that his bill hadn't been paid. The hero would have noticed all this, noticed too the piebald blue velvet curtains and warm blue Axminster carpet and the odd effect of large gold cufflinks on the specialist's rather grubby white cuffs. He would have noticed all this and would have been in the act of putting it by for future use; and then he would have realized that there wouldn't be any future.

That's where I would have started. There would have been his great love, his one and last love. He would have wanted to spend as much time as possible with her. He wouldn't have wanted to spend any time at all with his wife because she didn't love him. But he would also have wanted to have spent as much time as possible with his children. He would also have needed to finish a book, because he would have needed money, because he was broke on a large scale. He would have needed the money for the children. It would have been a package deal: he would also need the money for his wife. And he couldn't be with the children unless he was also with his wife.

So there you have it: he'd be torn two ways, in fact more than two ways. He'd want to go home to Yorkshire too and see his family and friends. He'd want to use the time left to him – maybe a year, maybe eighteen months – to the fullest. I don't mean that there'd be a frantic search for pleasure, but he'd want love and he'd want art. And he'd want to write a book into which he put the whole of himself. Some clerical idiot once saw St John Bosco playing billiards. 'How frivolous an occupation for a priest!' he exclaimed. 'What would you do if you were to die an hour from now?' 'Finish my game of billiards to the greater glory of God,' the saint replied. There'd have been that in my novel too: the hero would have finished his book to the greater glory of God.

This is only by way of illustration. All that he would have cared about would have been finishing the book. God doesn't really come into it. Not that one can be ever quite certain: God makes no appointments, lets Himself in, and doesn't care what inconvenience He causes. That could have been something extra, something quite unpredictable. It doesn't really affect the central theme of the man who's trying to cram everything into a brief period, trying to tell his story and live it too. The objection was that it was too neat, too tidy, too professional, it had been done too often before. And somehow or other I would have distanced myself too much from the hero, I would yet again have avoided telling the truth about myself. Which would mean that I'd never tell you the truth about yourself.

I owe you, my readers, that. I've grown so much since I've met Vivien – I can't help repeating this, there's no other way. I never understood before I met her how much I've had from you, how much I'm in your debt. And though I haven't had a death sentence pronounced upon me in Harley Street, I don't feel that I've all that much time left. I've been a bit too thrifty with my material, I've been saving it all up and now there's an overabundance of it.

And time is passing by me now. Once, some five years

ago, during the period of displacement, during the worst period of my life, I didn't know how to get through the days. Drink was the only thing which would help me dispose of time. I had been robbed not only of sex but of physical affection and tenderness and I realized that this was the magic ingredient which kept my marriage, with all its imperfections, alive, and what made me welcome every new day. And now every new day was a burden and I longed for sleep, and I was displaced, wandering and lost.

Then from the first moment I met Vivien time passed quickly. Once – it must have been about our sixth meeting – we had coffee at the Festival Hall at one-thirty and the next time I looked at my watch it was half-past five. We hadn't even thought of lunch. I can't remember what we talked about. (Let me have a little tranquillity, an hour with the pressure off, and I'll recapitulate every word.) We didn't hold hands or kiss or have any concrete sexual intentions or make any big decision. We just talked without stopping and it was as in those old films when the clock hands whiz round. It's still like that.

Now thinking only of myself, I add that it's not the hours I spend with her that I'm thinking about. I accept – we both accept – that I can't live only for myself. If I have been given more, I have a duty to give more.

I have much more too. The time I spend with Vivien is the perfect time, when every sense is heightened, when I have come to realize how much happiness a man and a woman can give each other. But it irradiates the rest of my life, the time spent apart from her. And more and more joyfully – quietly but joyfully – I've become grateful for what I have. For a start, there's my five-bedroomed and two-bathroomed red-brick house in Boxley, a commuter town, roughly equidistant from Woking and Weybridge, about forty-five minutes from Waterloo. There's nothing much to say about the house, which has bay windows on the ground floor and a grey slate roof and a dormer window in the loft, except that it has never offended anyone's eye. The rooms are large and, as in Raymond's flat off Shaftesbury Avenue, the proportions are right. It was built in 1924, it's about the same age as me, and it has worn well and is in good shape. The workmanship is superb, the timber seasoned and the bricks have mellowed beautifully over the years. And there's one third of an acre of tolerably well-kept garden – mostly lawn, with roses and shrubs and apple trees and pear trees and a big garden hut at the bottom which the children have taken over as a playhouse.

There's nothing much to say about Boxley either. It's clean and undistinguished and prosperous, though these days there's a chill wind blowing which I imagine started from the Middle East. There aren't quite as many two-car families, a few shops have closed down, middle-aged executives are finding themselves redundant, people are eating mince instead of steak and wondering what the hell they're going to do when they can't afford mince. But the wind is merely chill, not icily penetrating, as in the North. Boxley has a bad cold, but the North is heading for pneumonia.

I'm not, of course, making any judgements here. I'm not condemning Boxley. I honestly am grateful to be living in Boxley. Wouldn't any poor devil in the front line be glad to be at HQ if he got the chance? I don't really go in very much for moral judgements or, to be really modish, value judgements. I'm concerned only with things as they are, not in the least with how they should be.

You have to know me before I can tell you my story. I wasn't born just as I am now at the age of fifty-six. I have a past which has made me as I am, and you must know something of that past, but not all of it.

But for the moment never mind about the house, Surrey, the white Granada Ghia estate car, my gold Rolex Oyster and gold identity bracelet, my trips to London and New York and Leningrad and Warsaw and Amsterdam and Sydney and Los Angeles and Paris, de luxe all the way. Never mind about the grand and glittering parties, never mind about the unfailing pleasure of being recognized and

35

lionized. That's all part of my life and I have enjoyed it. Don't expect me to tell you that all is vanity, that success turns to dust and ashes in the mouth. It doesn't. The taste of dust and ashes is the taste of failure. Better to be a living dog than a dead lion: but better still to be a living lion than a living dog.

I was taught by Jesuits and had a good Irish Catholic mother, and I have an uneasy feeling – yes, it's here again – that in amongst the theology and the ritual there's a huge and disruptive force that would have no compunction about messing up my whole life. I don't have this feeling very often, and words like *huge* and *disruptive* and *compunction* come nowhere near describing it. *Who knoweth what is good for man in this life, all the days of his vain life which he spendeth as a shadow? For who can tell a man what shall be after him under the sun?* Very well, my life may have been a vain one, but I have not spent it as a shadow.

We'll put this aside for a moment. I am what I am because I was born in Casterley and lived there – apart from a break of two years in the Army – up to the age of thirty-one. Casterley is part of me. Casterley is always with me, though I don't think that I'll ever live there again.

Then there are the people – my father, my mother, my sisters, my first wife, my second wife, my children, my friends, my relations. I daren't at this point even name them. They're all there in my mind, even the dead ones, even those I haven't seen for years. My Irish relations are a particular problem. The other people in my life don't push themselves forward. They enter only upon invitation. But my Irish relations have established squatters' rights.

My Irish relations are always there. They are even in my dreams. I scarcely ever dream of my English relations. It doesn't make any difference whether the Irish relations are alive or dead, whether I've seen them recently or haven't seen them for years. It doesn't make any difference whether I like them or not. I don't believe that they actually like me. I don't believe that they really like anyone except their own

36

immediate family. They do, of course, pour on the old Irish charm whenever we meet, but I'm impervious to it. Those whom I liked the best were Black Irish; they're now all dead. My mother and her brother, my Uncle Thaddeus, were Black Irish. The Black Irish are bitter and sardonic and always speak their mind. They just don't blurt it out, and they haven't any burning interest in justice. Not being stupid, they know that there isn't any. It's simply that they don't like pretension. And they have a sense of humour; which has nothing to do with telling jokes. Neither has it anything to do with laughing easily. In fact, the Black Irish rarely laugh. The other kind of Irish, the Dreamers, never know whether to take them seriously or not. But from time to time they realize that the Black Irish aren't taking them seriously and then, if they're in a position to do so, they kill them. Michael Collins and Kevin O'Higgins were Black Irish. If the IRA hadn't killed them the Free Staters would have done.

But I shall keep them in their place. I'm setting down honestly a real love story. And I can see now that everything that happened to me before I met her was leading me towards her. She is all that I ever wanted in a woman. No, I'm not being romantic. I'm telling you the plain facts. Love is as real as hate, happiness is as real as depression. This is going to be a happy story. It has a happy beginning and it will have a happy ending.

There's nothing one can't reveal these days. I don't in the least mind admitting that. I'm selfish, arrogant, self-centred and, as Vivien rightly said, spoilt. I've been spoilt all my life. I've been made a fuss of, I've been taken notice of. I've been lionized, I'm used to being the entre of attention. I'm a real prima donna. And until I met Vivien I'd taken more love than I'd given.

I admit all this and am prepared to admit even more, almost with a sense of pride. But what I'm almost prudish about, what I find it difficult to admit is this: what I feel for Vivien is a pure and unselfish love. Since knowing her, I have felt myself changing. I'm not about to become a saint, but I'm growing into someone resembling a decent and mature human being. And now I understand what Lenin felt when he listened to Beethoven's *Apassionata*: 'Astonishing, superhuman music ... what miracles people can do... But I can't listen often to music, it affects my nerves, make me want to say kind stupidities and pat the heads of people who, living in this dirty hell, can create such beauty. But now one must not pat anyone's little head – they would bite off your hand, and one has to beat their little heads, beat mercilessly, although ideally we're against any sort of force against people. Hmm – it's a devilishly difficult task.' I'm going to listen to the *Apassionata*.

Three

In the words of the old Methodist hymn, *A charge to keep have I*. A charge is a duty, a post to guard, a contract to honour. Here early one wet June evening, I'm in the sitting-room of my home trying to achieve some sort of detachment. I appear to be reading the *Sunday Telegraph* but that's only so Val won't ask me what's the matter. If I'm not reading or writing or watching the TV she tends to panic. *What's the matter?* is a simple enough query but she always manages to cram into it a note of rising hysteria. She can't accept that I might simply want to sit still and think in my huge armchair with the blue floral loose cover, part of a suite bought from Heal's some nineteen years ago and still as good as new.

I'm starting to make some sense out of my life. I said *starting*. The pattern's clearer than it was and the colours brighter, but things are far from being what they should be. To begin with, I don't want to look at Val. We haven't had a quarrel today and we haven't had a quarrel for a long time. She scarcely ever flares up any more, and when she does pulls herself together with a visible effort. When I become irritated she isn't exactly Patient Griselda, but rides the storm and doesn't harp on about it afterwards.

Not that that would have mattered once. I could have quarrelled with her all day, I could have been at the point of packing my bags and leaving her, I could have actually hated her. I could have been planning to open hostilities again, I could have been choosing with care words which would have hurt her as much as her words had hurt me.

39

And I still would have wanted to look at her. I have always enjoyed looking at her from the time I first met her, some twenty-two years ago. (I married her the year after.) She is in fact good-looking, ash-blonde with startlingly blue eyes but dark eyebrows and eyelashes, neat features and a full mouth. It's held tighter now than ever it has been; the lines are deepening from the base of the nose. Ten years more and they'll be as harsh as mine. She's tall – five foot six – and slim, with small breasts which are, whilst being in proportion, surprisingly exuberant. And she has marvellous legs. And that's enough of that: she's a person, not a collection of parts.

I'm trying not to look at her. Some years ago I'd look at her and enjoy looking at her and we'd go to bed early and lock the door. But then there was some point in looking at her. There isn't now. She's just finished knitting a pale blue sweater for Vanessa. She's put it down for a moment to take a sip from the glass of red wine beside her. She rarely smokes: wine is her chief indulgence. A glass of wine, not vintage but a shade better than plonk, lasts her all evening. She's wearing a button-through denim dress, and her legs are bare. She's not sitting carelessly but the dress only just covers her knees and the bottom button begins about six inches up. The neck is shirt-style; it doesn't go down as far as the cleft between her breasts, but she fiddles with the button absently. I don't know how I've taken all this in; I'm not looking, I don't want to look. You needn't feel sorry for me, and I don't feel sorry for myself and I'm here in this room of my own choice. I have to show her to you. But I don't want to have her around at the moment.

Why am I here? Not only in this house, but in this room? There is a study where I have a comfortable armchair and a lot of books and a radio. The answer to both questions is my son Simon and my daughters Penelope and Vanessa. Simon is eighteen, Penelope thirteen, and Vanessa twelve. Simon's a bit over six foot, slim like his mother, not with an Irish navvy's build like mine. He has fair hair like his mother. But his face is more unguarded. Val's face is becoming, when she's out in the world, having to acknowledge the existence of other people, increasingly alert, ready to take cover or, to attack. I've seen that look on men's faces behind the enemy lines. It's not an expression that a civilian should wear.

Simon has a civilian face – come to think of it, an English face. Penelope has blue eyes and fair hair, there's Irish somewhere in her face, a wildness and a bluntness, bluntness in the sense of there being a fraction less curve, a fraction less softness than one would expect. I think she'll be as tall as her mother. In one way she reminds me of Vivien: her face is unafraid. Not aggressive, unafraid. She too would walk up to the cannon's mouth. Vanessa has blue eyes, but grey-blue like mine. And she has black hair like my mother; but oddly enough, not much trace of the Irish. She's the gentlest of the three, gentler than Simon, who can flare out savagely from time to time. I have, however, a suspicion that she's also the toughest. She's sturdier than Penelope, not fat, not stocky, but with larger bones. She's not clumsy, she's all in proportion but she is, in a word, foursquare.

The three of them aren't at this moment speaking. Vanessa is lying on the sofa looking at the *Sunday Times* colour supplement in a happy trance. Penelope is sewing a stitch on a pair of jeans. She's sitting on the upholstered window seat. The rain beats against the window; it's not very warm. The bay window overlooks the front garden. There's two entrances and a broad gravel drive with a privet hedge on the left and a new ranch-type fence on the right. There's a decent-sized lawn and a garden seat and flower-beds at the front. It's not as big as the back garden but it's big enough to stretch one's legs in without looking ridiculous.

There is often this frustration, always this tension between Val and myself, but I still enjoy being in this room. It's because my children are there. We agree about them, we agreed some time ago about the house and about the blue-green-and-cream Axminster fitted carpet, the

gunmetal-blue and smoke-grey flowered Sanderson curtains, the Heal's suite, the leather buttoned sofa on the left, the
gas fire, the teak nesting tables, the long cream-tiled coffee
table, even the magazine rack. And there are four paintings
of Casterley by my friend Roy Alfreton which we chose together. There's a set of wall units in teak, but there are only
two book sections. Most of my books are in my study and
my office. The walls are plain cream: we have tried pat-
terned wallpaper, but it somehow is too fussy for this room.

I like this room, but I'm not deeply fond of it. I'm not
deeply fond of the house. But then I've never loved houses.
I've loved places and people, never houses. Val loves this
house and she loves the children. She loves her father and
her mother and her sister and her brother. I don't think that
she loves places. As if she knows that I am thinking about
her, she looks towards me.

'Are you going away next week?'

'I told you. I have to go to Wetherford to do a broadcast.
Tuesday.'

'You didn't tell me.' She frowns. 'Never mind.'

'I did tell you. But what haven't I to mind?' My irritation
is growing. There's a chance of my controlling it now; there
wouldn't have been once.

'I was thinking of having the Mintlakes in for a drink.
And perhaps the Fitzpatricks. Never mind.'

'We can have them in some other evening.'

'It's not important. Are you staying with your father?'

'Of course I am. Godammit, I told you so!'

She shrugs; suddenly the edge has gone off her voice. 'All
right. Keep your hair on.' She turns to Vanessa, holding out
the sweater. 'Let's have a look at you, love.' She holds the
sweater against Vanessa. 'Yes. That's it. You'd better try it
on.'

'It's smashing, Mummy. Will the blue skirt go with it?'
Vanessa, like her sister, indeed like her mother, has a fresh,
clear voice, and no Surrey affectations; it's only just left
childhood.

'I don't really think so. That skirt's too light. You don't have the contrast.'

'The black one might do. The check one.'

'You're too fat. It doesn't fit.' Penelope sticks her tongue out at Vanessa.

'Stop stirring, Penny,' Val says. 'Try the blue skirt, Vanessa.'

Vanessa takes the sweater and leaves the room, tweaking Penelope's hair as she gets up. There's a brief scuffle.

'Stop it, or there'll be tears,' I say gruffly. 'Or something broken.' I'm now quite happy. There's this current of life in the room, there's youth and innocence, there's a feeling of being in the shoes of my daughters, every moment fizzing gold light, every moment like sparklers, to be held high or to be whirled around in golden circles. And that it's so undeniably there is because Val and I, no matter what else we've disagreed about, have always been of one mind on how to bring up the children. We both of us love them more than we love ourselves. And even that isn't being quite fair to Val: she put nothing before the children. Whereas if it came to the crunch for me, it's my work which would come first. If I were given to feeling guilty, I'd feel guilty about this. As it is, I've learned to live with it.

Simon gets up or rather unwinds himself from the sofa. 'I'm going over to Larry's.'

'When will you be back?' Val asks.

'About ten.' He yawns and stretches himself.

'Are you ready for tomorrow?'

'As ready as I ever will be. 'Bye.' He saunters out; the sitting-room door slams, the front door slams.

'He's a cool customer,' Val says. 'He never worries, does he?'

'If he does, he doesn't let it show.'

'He doesn't let anything show very much.'

'He's a bit dour at times.'

'He's a good boy!' Her voice is fierce.

'All right, all right. I'm not saying he isn't. No need to be emotional.' I'm trying hard to make my tone soothing.

'Don't you tell me not to be emotional!' There's a faint flush on her face, she's leaping into the attack. I close my eyes, feeling enormously tired and then Vanessa enters the room in her new sweater and Val switches herself off; or rather it's as if she has been switched off by someone else. She gets up and goes over to Vanessa and I go into the kitchen and take a can of lager out of the fridge.

The kitchen is large with vinyl floor tiles in amber and maroon, a big pine table and six matching chairs and pine matching units and a big pine cupboard. The wallpaper is speckled amber and orange, the curtains are plain yellow. There's a dishwasher, a deep freeze, a Kenwood mixer, an extractor fan, an electric double oven cooker, a disposal unit, a water softener: you name it, we have it. The laundry, a long narrow room, is next door, visible through two long windows in the kitchen wall.

All this is important. The rain has stopped; I open the back door and smell the wonderful freshness. This is important too. There's always this fresh smell after rain, but in Surrey, I feel, it's fresher than anywhere else, because there are more trees, more grass, more flowers. As I think this I'm saying it to Vivien too. She understand about the fresh smell after rain, just as she understands what I feel about the kitchen.

I close the door and take a glass from the cupboard and sit at the table. I stroke the smooth wood – smooth but giving the sensation that it lies in one direction like fur, that one could almost ruffle it – and try to think. This kitchen would easily accommodate the living-room and the kitchen of my father's house. That doesn't matter. Neither does it matter how much it all cost. And I don't see it as a success symbol. But none of it has to be taken for granted. I'm saying all this to Vivien, actually saying it under my breath. And then I realize that she isn't there, that she's some thirty miles away in Hampstead, and self-pity descends upon me. Descends? It's thrown over me, as in the arena. One gladiator has a net and trident, his opponent a sword. I'm struggling beneath the net now. I want to go back to the sitting-room to be with Vanessa and Penelope, but only to be with Vanessa and Penelope. I light a cigarette and am about to open the can of lager. Then I put it back into the fridge unopened and put the glass back in the cupboard. I have seen the trident. Self-pity and cold lager would add up to my waking up at noon tomorrow with an aching head and a sense of guilt and impending doom and, what is even worse, no work done that day. I return to the sitting-room.

'Anybody for tea?'

Val smiles. 'Yes, please, Daddy.' That's the sign that there'll be no trouble. Five years ago, I'd jokingly call her 'Mother', pronouncing it the Yorkshire way, and she'd call me Father, also pronouncing it the Yorkshire way, which is 'Feyther'. It was a private joke; what it meant was that we still had sex, that we still had a marriage. *Daddy* is different: in a strange way it sometimes almost makes me feel that she is my daughter and I know very well that she isn't. And yet I feel that it's a sign of goodwill towards me, that it somehow proves that there's affection somewhere, that against all the odds the marriage continues.

When I'm drinking my tea, Vanessa comes over and sits on the arm of my chair. 'That scarf and shirt look very well together, Daddy,' she said. The scarf is red silk from Sulka's, the shirt a flecked blue linen from Austin Reed's. I've had them a long time. I believe that all men's throats – and chests too – should be covered up past forty.

'I'm glad you've noticed them, darling,' I said.

She strokes my hair. 'You've wonderful crisp hair, Daddy.'

I can't restrain a smirk. 'So people tell me.'

Val smiles indulgently. 'She's after something, Daddy.'

'I know.' I tweak Vanessa's hair gently. 'An advance on your clothing allowance. Yes?'

All right, then, this is what I have. I'm saying this to Vivien now, for she will understand. I'm with my children now and I'm with my children most days. No, I'm not their buddy, I'm not a family man, I am not a domestic animal. I pay my bills, I keep the law. I meet my deadlines, I turn up to all my appointments dead on time. But I'll never potter round in a cardigan and old trousers and down-at-heel shoes, puffing an old smelly pipe. I'm not just a big child myself, but I haven't stopped growing. And suddenly there's an epiphany. Everything is in the proper order and the proper place. There are four human beings in this room and all sorts of objects – newspapers, ornaments, furniture, books, bottles of gin and whisky and martini and brandy and rum and sherry, glasses and ornaments and pictures, a pair of jeans and Vanessa's sweater, the wooden tea-tray and the tea-things – and it's like a Japanese flower arrangement. This was ordered for someone's pleasure: being an epiphany, it is joyful, it opens out, but it is also austere and restrained. The flowers are the children; flowers aren't easy to come by. A Japanese flower arrangement isn't just flowers. All else but the children are the heaps of dry, silvery sand, smooth pebbles, loosely tied little bundles of brightly dyed grass.

Vanessa is promised her advance and presently I go to my study to write my *Argus* review. There's not much to say about my study: it's half the size of the sitting-room, with mustard-coloured fitted carpet, fitted bookshelves round three walls, a blue studio couch with a big red and yellow and blue mohair rug folded over it, a small electric fire, a small battered elm office desk, a large elm cupboard, a revolving office chair, a small and a large coffee table, and a large battered wing chair in piebald beige moquette. I only write my reviews and odd letters there.

My desk overlooks the back garden which, like the front, is mostly lawn. The two crabapple trees at the bottom of the garden are in bloom, pink and white, and there's a tangle of hawthorn next to them, only just beginning to bloom. Later it'll be all white. Presently I won't see the garden or the room, only what I'm writing.

This evening the epiphany comes between me and the review. I want to hang on to it. I hope for a surge of epiphanies, I want to sit quiet and grow; and then, as always, I start writing, and at some point the garden is darkening and I'm switching on the light and there is no sound, no other people.

And now I've put the piece down – I write in stiff-backed lined writing-books – and have leaned back in my armchair. I look at my watch. It's half-past ten. Vanessa and Penelope enter in their dressing-gowns to say goodnight. This isn't an epiphany, nor does it make me a family man. But if there really is to be an accounting for my life I'll be able to say that I used this moment well, as I used the two and a half hours before it well, that I wasted none of it, that I kissed my daughters goodnight and felt towards them a pure and warm and uncomplicated animal affection. That's good enough, that's more than a lot of people have during the whole of their lives.

I go into the kitchen for a can of lager. My work for the day is done; the arena is empty. Val is there in her dressing-gown making a pot of tea. There's a tray with milk jug and a mug on the table. There would have been two mugs once.

'Have you finished?'

'With an effort. Never mind, it's a hundred quid for two and a half hours. Nearly fifty quid an hour ...'

My voice trails off. She's not really interested. She doesn't read the pieces. She hasn't read any of my books for a long time; my temper is rising, and then I see the net. With an effort I distance myself.

She crushes the teabags down with a spoon and puts the teapot on the tray.

'Simon phoned. He'll be in about eleven. Are you going to bed now?' Her tone is bright, friendly, matter-of-fact.

'I have some notes to make. I'm going to Deira TV tomorrow.'

'Are you passing by a bookshop? You could get something for mother. You always know what she likes.'

'I'll drop them in on my way home.' I look at her sharply; her shoulders now are drooping, she looks suddenly older. 'Isn't she well?'

'She's had to go back to bed. I phoned this evening. Father says it's probably the new tablets.'

'You should have told me.'

'I know you were busy. I'll pop in tomorrow anyway.'

She looks as if she wants to cry and all of a sudden I'm transfixed by a terrible pity. Once she would have cried and I'd have put my arms around her and comforted her. It wouldn't necessarily have ended in sex; why should it? But now, because there isn't any sex, there can't be any physical affection and she must weep alone.

'I'm sorry. I know you must be worried.'

She straightens her shoulders. 'I don't want to tell the kids too much, particularly Simon. He'll have enough on his mind. She'll be glad to see you.' She hesitates. 'You're a rotten sod sometimes, but you're good with sick people.'

'I'm glad I have some virtues.' I keep my voice gentle.

'Oh yes. You're not all bad...' Her voice trails away. She yawns. 'Oh God, I'm *whacked*. Goodnight, Daddy.'

'Goodnight.' I sit down suddenly on the nearest chair: it's as if all the strength has been drained out of me.

I'm now in the dining-room of her parents' house at tea the Sunday before, high tea rather than afternoon tea with every possible variety of cold meat and a huge bowl of salad and hot sausage rolls and a hot *quiche lorraine* and chocolate cake and cream cake and fruit cake and chocolate biscuits and a bowl of trifle and a huge pot of strong tea. Vanessa and Penelope and Simon are still eating, but Val's father has lit his pipe and Val and I have lit cigarettes. It's a bright afternoon and there's a view of the garden through the French windows. It's a substantial red-brick detached house on a small estate in Weirton about two miles away from our house and about three hundred yards away from Val's father's shop, which sells newspapers and magazines

48

and sweets and tobacco and stationery and has been doing very well for a very long time. Val's father is of medium height, sturdy, placid, balding now, with a square fresh-complexioned indefinably English face. He's a very neat man, neat as his home is neat and his garden is neat and his shop is neat, always wearing a good suit and a clean shirt and tie and his shoes shining and never down at heel. He was, of all things, a bomber pilot in the war. He helped me with the background for my first novel. His wife, who is fair like Val, is grey now but she isn't as plump or as rosy as she was, her blue eyes seem a little puzzled, even hurt, as if someone for no good reason has threatened to strike her. She hasn't eaten very much, but she's drinking her tea thirstily. The room is fresh and clean in grey and pink and eggshell blue shades and there are flowers everywhere. I've always felt at home in the house of my in-laws and have always been made welcome there.

'You take my advice, Simon,' my father-in-law is saying. 'Go into local government or the Civil Service. Don't be self-employed. It's nothing but worry –'

I laugh. 'You've never worried in all of your life, you old devil,' I say affectionately. 'You'd go mad working for someone else.'

And then I look at my mother-in-law, who's talking to Val about the cost of food. Val has just paid over four pounds for a piece of beef which was only just enough for the five of us. It's all very soothing, it's not to be taken all that seriously and yet it's a source of strength to me. For myself I prefer the company of the *gens du monde*, the people of the world. I am a high-flyer, a metropolitan man. But a deep need in me is answered by high tea in the suburbs with Val and the children and my father-in-law and mother-in-law, and I want this part of my life always to be the same. And now my mother-in-law says, 'They're fine children. You should be glad they've got good appetites. Look at Rosie Sanders –' and I can fill in what she's going to say, about the next-door neighbours' daughter who nearly died of anorexia nervosa, but she's stopped and is gasping for breath. Val is up from her chair and then her mother has recovered her breath, the crisis is over and we hear all about Rosie Sanders, but I've seen the blow threatened again, and I see change on the way. I've always seen this house as a fortress, but a siege is coming none can withstand.

And I put it out of my mind. I hold only this in my mind: there are many different kinds of love. At one and the same time I'm grateful for it and I feel imprisoned by it. With an effort I turn my attention to my notes in front of me. I lose myself in them. Then I sip my lager and look them over, reflecting with a certain arrogance that I'm a damned good writer. Yes. I'm calm. Yes, I'm happy. And all these thoughts I'm saving up for Vivien. They're not particularly profound, or original, but she'll be interested, she'll share. As long as I live this sharing will continue, this friendship, this civilized and sane but warmly lively delight. And then, with no warning, I'm back, some five years back in bed with Val in the room we used to share, with the rather flashy blue and gold striped fleck wallpaper and the thick blue fitted carpet and the *en suite* bathroom we had put in. It's the bed that matters, though, the king-size bed with the Dunlopillo mattress and the blue quilted continental bedhead, the bed where Vanessa and Penelope were begotten.

It's summer, it's been a long hot day, it's going on for midnight and it still isn't cool. In those days I felt the heat more because I was a stone heavier. My pyjama jacket is soaked in sweat, and I've just thrown it on the floor. I've drunk my Ovaltine and a glass of iced water, closed my book – I'm re-reading *The Silver Chair* – and I've smoked a last cigarette. This is the routine: half-an-hour's reading, the Ovaltine and the iced water, a couple of cigarettes, lights off. Val reads too – generally historical novels by writers like Jean Plaidy – and sips a glass of red wine. I've never known her to take more than one glass of wine. She's wearing a Laura Ashley cotton nightdress, high-necked with ruffles, Victorian style, very prim and proper and absolutely opaque, but I can see the shape of her breasts very plainly and my erection begins.

'I'm going to put the light off,' I say to her. 'OK?' I smile at her. 'That nightie suits you. Very demure.'

She doesn't seem to have heard. She puts her book down. 'Can't get on with this book. I think I've gone off her.'

'You asked me for it.'

'Very kind of you.' She snaps out the words. 'You can put the light out.'

There's a full moon, which makes the room seem bigger than ever. We chose a bold pattern to make it a little cosier and of course the bathroom takes a corner off, but it doesn't seem to have made any difference. It's a strange room – I don't mean that it's haunted or anything of that nature, but just that it's quieter than the other rooms. Even when, a long time ago, the girls were in, climbing all over us in the morning, making the din that small children do make, it was quieter than the other rooms were when they were empty.

I had never noticed this quietness so much as that evening some five years ago. Val's back is turned towards me, there seems somehow a great deal of distance between us. I put my hand gently on her shoulder to turn her round. Once that would have been enough. Now she knocks my hand away.

'I want to sleep.'

'Again? You always bloody well do these days.'

'I really am tired, Tim.'

'Have you got a headache too?'

'As a matter of fact, I have. Not that I expect any sympathy from you.'

'For Christ's sake, it's been three months. Bloody nearly four! What the hell's up?'

'Leave me alone. Haven't you any heart?' There's a note in her voice which, for the first time in my life, makes me seriously want to hit a woman.

'What the fucking hell has me having no heart to do with

it? What the fucking hell am I doing wrong?'

She sits up in bed suddenly. 'You're determined not to let me rest, aren't you?' Her face is tanned from our holiday in Spain but it now is really pale under the tan: not all that far, I note with a detached interest, from grey. 'Don't you remember? Don't you remember all the trouble I had after Simon? And after Penelope? And after Vanessa? And don't you remember what happened four months ago?'

'Yes, yes, yes!' I light a cigarette. 'You've got over it now, surely to God!'

'I nearly bled to death.'

'Yes, but you didn't. You told me that Robinson said you were all right.'

'You might make some tea, since you're determined not to let me sleep.'

I get out of bed and switch on the electric kettle which we keep beside the bed, and put teabags into the teapot beside it. I'm trying to keep my temper. 'Look, all I'm saying is that we can't keep on like this. We've got to come to some sort of understanding. I mean, I realize you've had a rough time. Well, see Robinson again. See anyone you like. Christ, I'm not a barbarian. I'm just a normal man.'

'Oh, you're that all right. Oh yes, you're a normal man all right. I'm just a hole to you!' She's nearly screaming now.

'Just a hole? Why, yes. Apart from that, what else have you to offer?'

She's out of the bed, her hand raised. 'You bastard!'

Now I'm angry. She's about to hit me: this is the one thing I can't stand. 'Calm down. It's a joke. A quotation.' I hold her eyes with mine. 'Have some tea, I won't make any more jokes.'

She returns to bed. 'Give me a cigarette.'

'Are you serious? It's twenty years since you had a cigarette.'

'I've had one from time to time. These last four months. Just give me one. I don't have to justify myself to you.'

'No.' I feel very tired. I give her the packet: she takes out a cigarette and I light it with my Dunhill. It's eighteen years since I saw her smoking: she gave up before she had Simon. 'No, you don't have to justify yourself. You never have done. Why should you change now?' I make the tea.

'You don't own me, you know.' She exhales noisily. She's a very noisy smoker: I'd forgotten how annoying this can be. Her inhalation is just as noisy too.

'I don't want to own you. I only want what's reasonable. I only want what's normal.'

'Like me nearly dying?' She accepts the cup of tea from me.

'Oh, Jesus, you don't have to freak out,' I say wearily. 'I don't understand you. You decide to have no more sex, you say nothing about it but just keep on making excuses. What the hell did you expect me to do? Go on, tell me.'

'Don't you dare to cross-examine me!' She's now trying to assume a cool dignity.

'Something's brought it on.' I'm sitting on the edge of the bed, my feet on the floor: I'm literally beginning to feel dizzy. I've had nothing to drink except two glasses of lager, but the bed doesn't feel steady, the room is on the verge of moving.

'Oh yes. Something has. That clever article of yours in the *Argus*. A writer is a man who keeps a notebook under his pillow on his wedding night. Oh yes. Very clever. All my friends have told me about it.'

'The tiny percentage who can read, you mean?' I finish my cup of tea, still feeling dizzy. 'But what the hell has it to do with us?'

'What has it to do with us!' She really is screaming now, her face darkly flushed. 'I'm your wife, aren't I? What are people to think?'

'What do I care?' I'm not dizzy any longer. I stand up. 'I don't give a damn what any of your peasant friends think. I don't give a damn about what *anyone* thinks. But what the hell does it have to do with our sex life? It's just words, that's all. It's a generalization. It's a little joke. It's nothing to do with you, and not all that much to do with me ...' My voice trails away. She isn't listening.

My problem now, after having shared four years with Vivien, is that when I look back I can't believe it. I didn't believe it at the time, I didn't believe in the reality of what I was hearing. I can believe in the reality of any variation of sexual desire, any variation of desire for money or power or fame or anything that's considered desirable. There isn't any human desire that I don't understand, though to understand all is emphatically not to forgive all in some cases. But what was Val after five years ago? What did she hope to gain from it? What has she gained now, five years after? And the answer is simple. I'm here, am I not, being a good provider, leaving home four mornings a week at nine am, coming home at five pm, being not only an exemplary father but an exemplary father figure? And she is safe in this well-made house with the well-made furniture, she has her own small circle of friends, nourishing and tasty meals are served at the appointed times, there's unlimited hot water and everyone has a bath each day and clean linen every day, bills are paid regularly at the end of each month, the cheques are always honoured, her father and mother and married brother Kenneth and married sister Juliet and married cousin Pauline all live nearby. And, above all, she has the three children.

And she has her friends, in particular the Mintlakes and the Fitzpatricks. Ernest Mintlake is an estate agent, a tall square cheerful man with short grey hair. His wife's much shorter, but curiously like him, redhaired, round where he's square, and equally cheerful. Ted Fitzpatrick's a chartered accountant, tall and square too, but rather less cheerful. He always seems rather astounded each time we meet that I do most of my work in a rented office away from home. His wife is rather a charmer, with black hair and large brown eyes and a marvellous heart-shaped face. Val met them at a PTA meeting some three years ago. These are her chief friends and her representative friends. They're middle class, sensible, decent people, fond of a good dinner and a drop to drink but by no means dissipated, fond of a game of bridge but by no means gamblers: the men do their jobs well, the women run their homes well, they no doubt have their worries about money, but they will survive. I rather like them but take care what I say to them: they're more easily shocked than one would suppose. There are parties, there are dances, there are PTA meetings, there's the Townswomen's Guild and the Luncheon Club, there are coffee mornings and sherry mornings: Val's life is full, her world is Boxley and she's at ease in it. Whenever she has met my friends of the *gens du monde*, she hasn't been happy. Shirley, my first wife, would have been happy in my world: but in Casterley there's always been a tradition that class doesn't matter. It matters as much there as anywhere else, but the tradition remains. In Boxley, they're as frightened of mixing with people of what they consider to be above their class as they are of mixing with people of what they consider to be below their class. But however this may all be, Val is content.

And yet this isn't fair. She enjoys all the material things which I can give her; she'd be a fool if she didn't. But she didn't care whether I had any money or not when she first met me, and her parents helped us to buy our first house. I don't think that she'd care now if I had to lose all that I have. She wouldn't exactly exult over it, but she'd very cheerfully adapt herself to straitened circumstances. For then she'd be as important as me, she'd be my equal and more than my equal. We'd then be nearer the people we were when first I married her.

This is mere speculation. What matters is that now everything has settled down. There is no scandal and no fuss: the time of displacement is over. I come home sober or if I think I'm not going to, phone Val before midnight to tell her I won't be home till morning. It's rarely that anything is said, it's rarely that there are any scenes. As my mother used to say, the grass grows green over the battlefield. And for over four years, except for the occasions whenever we've had a houseful of guests, we've had separate rooms. She keeps our old room, the biggest bedroom, the bedroom with the bathroom *en suite*, the bedroom where I begat my three children. I haven't been in it above three times since I started to sleep in what used to be the spare room. And on each of those occasions I've been visited by a frightening hatred, an anger that has left me totally exhausted and literally sick.

And now I'm back on that dreadful night again, realizing that she's not listening. That's all that I do realize: I've lived with her for twenty years and don't know her. I keep repeating this again and again. I don't know her, she's a complete mystery to me. She isn't now, after four years shared with Vivien, after four years with a reasonable being. Now I recognize the fact that not only was she not listening to me that night, she wasn't even seeing me as anything other than an arrangement of molecules, like the bed or the dressing-table or the fitted carpet.

If I had to present that scene from five years ago on TV now, I'd show the moonlight in pools on the blue carpet, the shadows black and jagged and dramatic, the reflections of moonlight on the dark wood of the furniture, my white towelling dressing-gown behind the door, the silver-backed brushes on the dressing-table, the silver-topped scent spray and the gold bracelet, gold necklet and pendant thrown down casually next to a pile of small change: I'd make the room very big and there'd be a pair of knickers and a bra thrown on the floor by the dressing-table, thrown with apparent carelessness but photographed so as to give male viewers at least some sort of *frisson*. I'd shoot the scene as it is but, in editing it, I'd cut away the figure of Tim and back it with black and bleep his words. She doesn't see me, she doesn't hear me.

Nothing like this goes through my head on that evening five years ago. I realize that she's not listening and stare at her.

'You're very cruel,' she says suddenly and surprisingly. 'You don't think of the effect on your children. You don't think how you make them suffer. Do you? Do you ever?' She spits out the words.

'What the fucking hell are you raving about?' I'm genuinely puzzled. I can't see any connection with what she's just been saying.

'Don't you know that their lives are a misery at school? Vanessa's friend Camilla told her that her Mummy said that you write dirty books.'

'Spare me this, will you? You'll have to put up with the way I earn a living. It's too late to change now even if I wanted to. The point is that you're going to wreck our marriage. Christ, I even thought it had been improving lately. Not that it was perfect, but that it was bearable.'

'Bearable! That is typical. Bloody typical!' She's nearly crying.

I shrug. 'You haven't been freaking out so much. We seem to have come to some sort of agreement. And after all there are the children. I'd put up with a lot for the sake of the children.'

'Oh yes. But you've a bad conscience there, haven't you? We all know about Kevin, don't we?'

'He's all right now. It's none of your business anyway.'

'He's all right if he keeps off the drugs.'

'He wasn't on drugs. He mixed with some horrible people, but he outgrew them.'

'Did he?' She shakes her head. 'You haven't heard the last of him.'

. 'I hope not. He's my son.'

'You should have thought of that when you let Shirley take him away.'

'I'm not going to argue with you.' I feel immensely tired: tired, not sleepy, empty, drained, defeated. 'Look, we'll talk about it tomorrow. I'm going to my study.' I take my dressing-gown from the hook on the door.

'Leave your cigarettes and lighter,' she says. Her tone is

quite matter-of-fact. I put them on the bedspread and go out without a word. She doesn't speak either.

There's a light on the landing as there always is. Simon at the far end of the landing, next to the bathroom, always keeps his bedroom door shut. Penelope and Vanessa sleep with their doors half-open, and only close them when undressing or dressing. Penelope and Vanessa's rooms are about three-quarters of the size of the main bedroom; they're still rather bigger than the double bedroom in the average modern house. Simon's at the front of the house is a shade smaller. Each has a substantial bed in pine, not double but rather larger than the average single. Val had a passion for pine when we bought them and a passion for the notion of plain white washable wall covering and no fuss. I look at Penelope's fair hair, fanned over the pillow; it's grown to just beneath her shoulders. The sunlight has made it very fair: it's a little darker in winter. Vanessa's hair is the same length but seems to stay all together: she sleeps curled up but with her arms at her sides. Penelope sleeps with her legs stretched straight out, but with her arms folded outside the sheets, as I do. No one told her to do this. Simon, I know, sleeps with his head pillowed on his arms, like Steerforth. There's something neat and orderly about this, just as his room is neat and orderly. Simon, once he left babyhood behind, made a deliberate decision to sleep switched off. The girls at the same stage let go, drifted, were taken over.

I stand at the door of Penelope's room, I stand at the door of Vanessa's room. I don't stand there for long; I wouldn't want them to wake up and see a white figure. But before I looked at each of them I was thinking in terms of a large Scotch, maybe two: after I have looked at them I'm thinking in terms of tea.

And now I'm in my study drinking tea. I don't know it, but the sense of displacement is beginning. The one or maybe two large Scotches would, of course, hold the displacement off, would keep things real, would put a comforting arm round me, but I might also finish the bottle, and then the next day there wouldn't be any work done, I'd just be sweating out a hangover and a sense of deep guilt and impending doom. The tea and three cigarettes at least are mildly soothing, almost convince me that everything is normal, that there's no crisis. Here these two tastes are, these two stupid but well-meaning and amiable friends standing beside me, always reliable, and for a while I listen to their consoling clichés: all women are odd, it might be her change of life, at least the children are there and the strawberries and raspberries and roses have done well this year... And it'll all blow over, because no one could be so unreasonable, because no one can just turn off sex after twenty years. After all, I say to her under my breath, it isn't as if you weren't keen on it. What do you think I'm going to do?

But it isn't quite as clear as all this, and the time it takes me to get as far as this is something like an hour. During the next three months I shall say all the things to her that I'm saying now, and a few more. Is there another man? My God, there's an explanation that fits! Go on, tell me. I promise not to do anything foolish. I've never hit you and I'm not going to start now. No? Honestly, you needn't be frightened to tell me. It can happen to anyone.

Now, the tea having gone cold, I lie on the studio couch and pull the mohair rug over me. I suddenly find my eyes close, I'm asleep, I'm weightless, I'm off in Casterley, there's a revue at the Little Theatre. I have a big part and I'm on stage and I don't know my lines. I'm looking out into the steeply raked auditorium and I've never seen it so full and there's another balcony above the balcony, but with red seats instead of blue, quite empty; and then I see Gillian. I was too young when I met Gillian to understand what love meant: she was first of all simply a woman twenty years older than myself, not to be thought of as a sexual being at all, then by stages a friend and companion and then suddenly and shockingly my mistress. And hasn't it always been the same story? I took more from her than I gave. And now

59

she's with me in the clearing by the stream in Wharton Woods and there's that dark moist marvellous surprise, the wonderful and delightful secret and those large soft breasts and her calm face suddenly calm no longer and the sound of the stream and thrusting joyfully – yes, the act has always been joyful to me – and yet with the thought my God I've done it now, I'm in for it now, there are footsteps coming, many footsteps, angry footsteps, and waking with the light still on and a spreading dark stain at my groin.

I actually feel extremely cheerful, full of male pride, and it's pleasant to think of Casterley. Wharton Woods is a small wood high above Casterley on the east with Casterley Moor behind it. There's a spring there a little way back from the main path: on the hottest day it's icy cold. And crystal clear: that's the only adjective for it, it's full of light, it's alive. I think it comes from Malham; and having thought that, I think of the old stone bridge at Malham and Malham Tarn, and the watercress I've gathered by the river there, watercress that is to the stuff one gets in the shops here in Surrey as kirsch is to vanilla essence. At Malham is the source of the River Aire, but it's a different river in the hills from in the valley. I think of Gillian and decide that now after all is the proper moment for one large Scotch – one, no more – and get up to take a glass from the cupboard and go into the kitchen for some ice. Gillian is now with me. Gillian my friend is keeping me company as I put ice cubes in the glass and return to my study and take the bottle of Johnnie Walker from the cupboard.

I don't return to the studio couch – which I haven't in any case bothered to let down – but sit in my armchair, the small coffee table on my right, and light a cigarette. I have matches and cigarettes here in the desk, but I remind myself to ask Val for my lighter back tomorrow. I take the drink very slowly. It's the best drink in the world, next to champagne, but only if taken slowly with plenty of ice. That was how Gillian taught me to take it. She taught me something about gesture too, and how to move across a stage and how to dress and, above all, how to speak. Up at the end of the sentence, darling, and speak from the diaphragm. And don't be frightened of speaking up. What else? You know what else. You know what was first. You know the title of my first book. That really says it all: she taught me the other things because she taught me about love in the first place. I had my lesson in love and everything else followed.

And thinking of her I begin to be aware of how much my life is askew. It's simply that I don't have any feeling of anyone being on my side. There doesn't seem to be anyone in whom I can confide. There isn't any sort of action I can take. I know the obvious action. I know that if Val means what she says, then I have grounds for divorce. And that means a small flat and loneliness, it means any amount of hassle, it means paying vast sums to lawyers, it means any amount of publicity of the precise kind which I've always avoided, sometimes more by good luck than good management. My first divorce only just made the local papers. And the situation was simple: Shirley had left me, taking Kevin with her. There wasn't anything to be done about that: action had been taken for me. And Kevin was only a year old, I was only just beginning to know him.

Excuses, excuses: I thought it wisest at the time not to see him, not to let him begin to know me, not to take the risk of his missing me. Jack, Shirley's new husband and my old friend, seemed kind enough, was perfectly willing to bring Kevin up as his own, even have him brought up as a Catholic if I so desired it. I thought it better not to burden the child with that either. And wasn't it the truth that I couldn't bear seeing Shirley with Jack, that I wanted to kill him and wasn't going to try it, since he was bigger and stronger and tougher than me?

And now I'm drinking for the wrong reason, for escape. I look at my watch: it's nearly six am, and I have a full day's work ahead of me, my new novel has, in the nick of time, begun to go smoothly. I'm up to two thousand words a day. I'll meet my deadline with a fortnight to spare, and if I meet my deadline I'll be able to reduce the overdraft and then if Larry means what he says there'll be the new TV series. I've only half-finished the whisky, but I take it into the kitchen, pour it down the sink, rinse the glass and put it in the dishwasher. Then I make myself some tea. I stay in the kitchen to drink it. There's a fresh breeze through the open window and I hear the birds. That's one of the best things about living in this country, and one of the best reasons for not living in France or Italy, where as soon as they see a bird (or for that matter any wild animal), they shoot it dead, with the result that in the morning, there's a strange silence.

There isn't another woman in my life except Val: my last affair, with a young actress called Marcia Wydenbrook, died a natural death some four months ago. In the first instance I discovered that she was as serious about her left-wing ideas as any actress can possibly be, in the next instance her ego was even larger than mine, and in the third instance she'd heard through the grapevine that my film deal hadn't come off. I'd talked to her about that film deal when first we met, but was stupid enough to assume that it was me she was interested in. It wasn't. She was terribly sympathetic – *Oh darling, I could cry for you* – and she did in fact cry, very becomingly, the tears filling her large violet eyes but not leaving them red afterwards, and since we were both in bed at the time, offered me some solid consolation and at dinner at the Imperia afterwards went through a list of all the friends – *real friends, dear heart, friends who love you as much as I love you, who know what an incredibly gifted writer you are* – but the large violet eyes were dry now and the words behind all this rubbish, the real message was: *Don't phone me, I'll phone you.*

So before the end of the evening I anticipated her by announcing that my American agent urgently wished to see me in New York and I had a lot of matters to clear up there, which wasn't strictly speaking true since what was really bothering me was that everyone in the USA seemed to have forgotten that I existed. So over the coffee and strega I was able to say quite casually that I'd be in touch on my return and I put her into a taxi and she laid her cheek against mine gracefully, her hands on my shoulders to show off her rings and heavy gold bracelet, one leg for a second flung up behind her to show off her leg and proclaim the fact of her being young, and went off to the King's Road, no doubt crossing out my name in her address book as soon as she got inside.

Not that she was cold-hearted as far as actresses go: an American actress would have got out of bed as soon as she'd heard I was a loser and have been dressed and out of the flat in a matter of minutes.

I have no right to feel sorry for myself: I live the life I've chosen to live, and I'm not keen on losers either. But I could have done without the extra burden of sexual frustration and was feeling rather aggrieved. Having almost made my mind up to be faithful to my wife and be a virtuous husband – for the sake of the children, I tell myself and almost believe it – it's hard that she should decide permanently to reject me. I suppose, to be honest, that I was getting tired of leaving a warm bed to go home and, though it always cossets a middle-aged man's vanity to be seen about with young women, I was beginning to feel that there's a certain lack of dignity about such relationships, that the young woman is out only for what she can get, that other men aren't really envious but faintly contemptuous, that there's no fool like an old fool.

It also occurs to me as I sit there in the kitchen drinking tea, that the young woman with an older man gets the best of it: she looks younger but he can only look older. As a consequence of the tea I go into the downstairs loo. Depression takes over, clutches me with bony hands. There is nothing, nothing now and nothing in the future, nothing I enjoy remembering, nothing I enjoy having now, nothing I look forward to enjoying in the future.

And I don't know why I exist or where I am. Of course my brain and eyes and ears and nose continue functioning, none of my senses is in the least deranged. But it's rather as if an old friend with whom one has always had a casual and relaxed and warm relationship suddenly became coldly correct and formal, addressed one as 'Mister' or 'Sir'. The smell of the soap is now simply the smell of scented soap, it doesn't make me think of crushing the dark smooth leaves of the lemon verbena in the garden at night. And the feeling of having clean hands – another tiny but real pleasure – has gone too. And when I return to my room and lie on the studio couch again I know that I won't sleep and I don't want to read and I don't want to listen to the radio and I don't want alcohol and I don't want tea. This isn't depression: it's worse.

Move on three weeks: it's evening and I'm in the lounge of the White Bear in Boxley, quite near my office. In my twenty-five years in Boxley I don't suppose that I've been there above twice. The pub in the centre of Boxley aren't to my taste: come to that, few pubs are. I've been working at home all day: Val has taken the children to the wedding of the daughter of an old friend of hers in Derbyshire, and is staying the night in Matlock. I've worked steadily all day, and now am certain that I can meet the deadline. I could go to London, there's bound to be a film or a play which I haven't seen. I could look up a friend. But I haven't the energy. I'd have to give something to the play or the film, something to a friend. And I have nothing more to give.

The lounge is large with stippled walls and oak panelling and a long oak panelling bar with a marble finish top. There are photos of Old Boxley, not that they're very old, because there wasn't really any Boxley before the railway came in the 1850s. There's a rather pretty barmaid in a low-cut blouse and two large barmen, both, oddly enough, with beards. They're all quite young and curiously classless. They don't have any sort of regional accent and both the men have freshly laundered white shirts. And they do look, as the saying goes, as if they could take care of themselves.

The lounge is crowded: it's Saturday night. There are a

lot of young people and even after two large Scotches they seem to me a dreary lot in their uniform of tight jeans and tatty shirts and tatty Indian print dresses and junk jewellery and hardly a decent complexion among them. I go to the bar and bring back a pint of lager which is described on the pump as chilled. It isn't, of course.

A young couple have come in and are seated on the other side of the alcove. The young man has short hair, a black blazer, grey flannels, brown suede shoes, a pencil-line moustache, a hard thin self-possessed face. The girl has black hair, a blue silk blouse, a blue-grey jacket and skirt, black court shoes, and marvellous long legs in black stockings.

Everything is clear up to this point. Then it becomes more and more confused. Displacement remains constant, the feeling of not belonging where I was but not belonging anywhere else either. Looking at the girl's legs is a well-established fact too. So also is the fact that they look as if they'd strayed in from out of the past: they wouldn't have been out of place in 1946 or even earlier. Another well-established fact is that there have been another four pints of lager, if not more. There is a haze too, and it's not all tobacco smoke.

What was said? At some time, I'm saying to the girl: 'You're physically attractive.' I'm aware of having said the wrong thing. I'm aware that neither of them is very high in the evolutionary scale. I'm aware of the young man's face contorted with rage. It makes him look rather silly and makes his moustache look false. I laugh at him. He throws a pint of lager in my face and half of it goes on my jacket.

And after this there is only me awakening at ten am on the studio couch in my study at home, fully dressed and with a blinding headache. I look at my shirt and jacket: there's no stain. The lager couldn't have been as weak as that. I look at my hands: the knuckles are cut and bruised. I stumble to the bathroom, strip, and inspect myself. There isn't a mark anywhere.

What happened? I don't know. I have never been to the White Bear or to any pub in Boxley again. And I don't think I mix in the same social circles as the habitués of the White Bear, so I'm never likely to find out. After that I did my drinking in London, mostly in Fleet Street. I'm not very proud of this part of my life and don't intend to tell you any more about it than I have to.

But there's one dialogue in our bedroom three weeks after the beginning of the time of displacement which I can't forget. I've come into the bedroom to collect some clean pyjamas. I'm now sleeping in the spare room

Val is sitting up in bed quite calmly reading a novel by Mary Renault.

I look at the book and feel so angry that I can hardly speak. 'Just tell me something, Val. Do you ever connect what you read with your own life?'

'It's just a story,' she says.

'It's about people,' I say, 'whether it's great literature or it isn't. It's about people with *feelings*, for Christ's sake!'

Then I literally double up as a spasm of pain hits my belly. I straighten up as the pain passes.

'You drink too much,' she says. 'And smoke too much.'

'Jesus, the wonder is I'm ever sober.' I sit on my side of the bed and light a cigarette. 'Listen, Val. How long are you going to keep this up?'

She's silent for a moment. 'I wish you'd let me have a bit of peace. You're the most selfish person I know.'

'Can't you see what it's doing to me? Can't you see how bloody frustrating it is?'

She sighs. 'Since you won't let me read, will you please let me go to sleep?'

'I won't argue with you. All right, you win. But can't you just admit that it's difficult for me? That's all. Just admit that. See things my way.'

'I suppose you want me to die,' she screams. She throws the book at me. It misses and lands on the floor. I stand up. It's throwing the book that makes me angriest of all, treating a book as if it were just any other object. I go out of the room. I'm totally off balance. I can't think straight any more. Because when I try to think straight I know that somewhere or other I must have gone wrong, that I haven't sufficiently acknowledged that it isn't her fault that she's different from me. I know that if I started from there, if I thought it all through, then somehow or other a solution might be reached. And then I realize that my thinking it through is no guarantee of her thinking it through, that she can't acknowledge that it's not my fault that I'm different from her. And then sheer fatigue intervenes. I go straight to my room, flop down on top of the bed and go straight off to sleep.

Four

A fortnight later I'm at Peter Rugeley's place in Hampstead, not far from Kenwood House. There's a new moon and when I get out of the taxi the house looks nearly as big as Kenwood House. It's Edwardian, in red brick which is nicely mellowed, an acre of gardens at the back – like mine, mostly lawn – and inside parquet floors, big rooms, long tables loaded with drinks and food and all over the house pictures which I keep telling myself can't be original, but which nevertheless I know very well are – four Andrew Wyeths, two Francis Bacons and a Chirico in the entrance hall alone. I like the way they're shown quite casually, I feel that Peter isn't a collector, they aren't trophies: he has bought the pictures because they give him pleasure.

As I hand my Burberry to the maid at the door, Peter bustles over towards me. He's of my age, give or take a year, with grey hair which is of a length both eminently suitable for a successful financier and for what used to be termed a dilettante, a little longer than Guards officers' length and a little shorter than artists' length. His suits are quiet, mostly in light grey and light blue, but he makes up for it with his shirts and ties which, if they weren't so obviously made to measure in Jermyn Street from the finest materials, one would call flashy. He's taller than me, and has my build, but it isn't the Irish navvy's build, more the English gentleman's, the rugger player's: it's all put together better, he moves with far more grace. His face is large and pink and smooth and he smiles readily: I don't think that he's had it lifted, but wouldn't swear that it hadn't been.

We've met from time to time at parties and once bumped into each other at a Buckingham Palace garden party. I'm here, I think, because recently I was temperately enthusiastic about his autobiography, largely because it was honest most of the time – though not all of the time, as the blurb implied. I haven't been to his home before, nor have I met his wife: we are acquaintances rather than friends.

He smiles when he sees me. 'My dear Tim, how good of you to come! Looking as young as ever, my dear chap.' He holds out both hands and squeezes mine. He isn't gay or even AC/DC: this, I've noticed from previous meetings, is near the top in his scale of greetings. There are a lot of people here but the house easily accommodates them all, and there's a smell of food and alcohol and flowers and cigars and perfume and, best of all, women. The sense of displacement is no longer with me, and autumn, my favourite season, is here.

'You're looking remarkably young too, Peter,' I say. 'It's the good clean life we lead.'

He laughs and pats my shoulder. 'Don't you believe it, my dear. It's all the luck of the draw.' He offers me a cigarette from a gold case. 'It's a question of metabolism. You're like me, you do what the hell you like and when you feel out of sorts you go to bed with soda water and Marie biscuits.' He looks at me thoughtfully, and pats my shoulder again. 'And yes, you're touchable. A problem for you, I'd say.'

'You're right.' For a moment I'm at a loss for words. It's a terrific personal PR job, an express delivery of a huge package of personal charm. He's been talking about me, he's been paying me compliments; at the same time he's been selling himself, he's been building me up, since he's also been talking about himself. 'Though it's bearable. Better than people moving away from one.'

He beckons a waiter over. 'You need a drink. Name your

desire, even though it may be for a pint of Tetley's bitter. We can even do that.'

'A dry martini. On the rocks. The vermouth saying hello to the gin. Twist of lemon.'

'The New York way?'

'The New York way.'

'You must meet my wife. That's her favourite.' A slim tall woman who might be thirty but probably is forty is suddenly there without having given the impression that she has been summoned, as the waiter was summoned. The impression given by that self-possessed but indefinably gamine face with the pointed chin and large startlingly blue eyes is that she's here in consequence of a whim, that she belongs only to herself.

'Lydia, Tim Harnforth. He likes bone-dry martinis too.'

'How do you do. Loved your thriller.'

I take her hand. 'How do you do. I'm glad you like it.' She's wearing a see-through blouse and no bra and tight pink velvet trousers. The breasts are small and round and firm with big nipples.

Peter smiles. 'You've laid the foundations for a meaningful relationship.' A young blonde billows towards him: I see now his true smile, not at all controlled, rather touchingly that of a little boy being given a Knickerbocker Glory. 'Excuse me, my dears.'

'His latest,' Lydia says, showing small white teeth wolfishly. The martini has somehow arrived and is in my hand; but I hate drinking standing up, which she somehow seems to understand, since we're now making our way without effort between couples who are dancing in what is almost a ballroom adjacent to the entrance hall and we're sitting on a large red buttoned leather sofa in a small room with pink fitted carpeting and walls covered with what appears to be beige suede. There's a long glass table in front of the sofa with a huge dark brown glass ashtray and a glass box full of cigarettes. Opposite is an identical sofa and table and ashtray. We're not at any great distance from the music but it's already distant, I'm glad to have it there, I'm pleasurably astounded that Lucy's in the sky with diamonds but I'm taking the first sip of the bone-dry Martini and the sense of displacement has gone. The drink is exactly right: it isn't straight gin but next door to it, and unless my palate misinforms me, it isn't the usual British gin: I sip again, and feel that the whole universe is wonderfully steady at last and all designed for my pleasure.

'I feel quite happy,' I say. 'A marvellous place you have here.'

'Too fucking marvellous. You saw Peter's blonde bit?'

'Dimly. I was looking at you.'

'Do you dye your hair?'

I begin to laugh, because already I'm liking her. 'Oh, love, honestly – do I look like it? Snip a bit off and have it analysed. Go on, I'll lend you my penknife.'

Two women have entered – or rather appeared in the room. One's blonde, in a wispy and short black dress showing off rather boldly two large pink breasts, the other brunette, at least ten years older, with a violet dress which appears to show rather more than the blonde's but in actuality shows virtually nothing at all. The blonde carries a blue cocktail, the brunette a multi-coloured cocktail – blue, yellow, green, orange. There are quick gestures of recognition in the direction of Lydia, smiles which aren't smiles but social grimaces. Then they turn towards each other. I don't think that now they're registering our presence at all.

Lydia glances at them, looks at me, and smiles tolerantly. She runs her hand through my hair: the gesture is surprisingly erotic. 'No, of course you don't dye it. It takes the spring out of it if you do.'

Her hair is light brown, approaching blonde, cut short in what used to be called the urchin cut. I touch it lightly. 'You don't dye yours either.'

'I help it along a little bit.' She takes two cigarettes from the box, lights them both with a gold lighter, and puts one in my mouth. 'You've been taking a bit of punishment lately, haven't you?'

'Christ, is it so obvious?'

'I don't mean you look ill. Just generally hassled.'

'I'm having trouble with a book.'

'Join the club. I'm having trouble with a book on Leningrad. Shouldn't have taken it on really.'

The brunette is now kissing the blonde, one hand on her waist, the other hand on her shoulder. The hand on the shoulder has prominent veins, long fingers, short nails, it's inclined to be scrawny, it's older than its owner's face. Darker too, all the more so because of the two huge rings, one emerald, one ruby, on the index and third finger and the platinum bracelet watch on the wrist. If you want to know a person's real age, look at their hands.

'Leningrad's the most beautiful city in the world. But it gets you down after a bit.'

'The St Petersburg *cafard*. Actually, you're very popular there.'

'Even despite *Pravda* officially designating me a fascist beast?'

'That was a long time ago. Who cares now? You're not all that political, are you?'

The brunette now is kissing the blonde's breast, her lips moving towards the nipple. Her left hand is out of sight. The blonde's eyes – large, blue-grey under dark eyebrows – are open very wide, the pupils dilated. Her lips are parted and she's breathing quickly.

'I used to be. Always making speeches, always sitting on some committee or other. Doesn't get you anywhere.' I have my eyes on Lydia's breasts: am I expected to gloat over them or am I expected to take them for granted? I now notice that she doesn't use scent, only some nursery kind of soap and talc with a faintly carbolic smell.

'I keep telling Peter that. He's done so much for the Tories – what have they done for him?'

'Perhaps they'll give him a title.'

'They'll want a lot more from him before they do that. I

wouldn't mind one myself. Anyway, it's pie in the sky right now.' The faint smell of nursery soap and talc doesn't mask her essential smell, which is very clean but clean as grass after rain is, as clean as an otter emerging from the river is, as clean as the wind over a high hill is.

'Pie in the sky often tastes better than the real thing.' I notice now what a clear unblemished skin she has, very fair, very smooth, very fine-textured. It's an English fairness: American women of that colouring always seem to me to have a tinge of sallowness and very often a fine peachlike fuzz. And Scandinavian blondes have a skin which is somehow thicker and more white.

She puts her hand on my thigh, quite near to my groin: it's a very warm hand, a strong square hand with the nails well-kept and short. 'Why are you looking at me like that?'

'I was thinking what a very English skin you have.' I put my hand for a moment very delicately on her cheek. 'Very fine, very pink and white, but not too damned delicate.'

She smiles, showing small white regular teeth. 'You have a nice skin yourself.'

'Oh, we're a handsome pair.' We're exploring each other very delicately, taking our places for the dance. And happiness – not in the least frenetic, not in the least tumescent – is entering. It's a very frivolous happiness, no commitments are being called for. We're ankle-deep. This is how I like it in the beginning, this is the approach of my generation. I'm not drunk, because even though I was unhappy when I came up to London, even though the displacement continued, Fleet Street and the atmosphere of the *Argus* office came to my aid. And I've been drinking this evening because I'm happy, which is the only proper reason to drink. And now there's the fact that I'm in business again sexually, that a woman desires me.

Why haven't I taken steps before now to get sex elsewhere? The answer is that for some twenty years sex has primarily meant sex with Val. Now that there isn't any sex with her, now that I'm in the habit of turning myself off sex, it's almost as if it weren't conceivable with anyone else. For all the unfaithfulnesses have never been any more than sporadic, I've always ended them as soon as there's been any chance of them becoming serious. Perhaps if only she would have overcome her mistrust of the *gens du monde* in the first instance, if only she'd been willing to share the sort of social life that I enjoyed, the unfaithfulnesses might never have occurred. Quite simply, I wouldn't have gone into the metropolitan jungle alone.

And now back in the time of displacement which, thanks to Fleet Street and alcohol and Lydia, is displacement no more, Peter bustles in, and descends upon the two women on the sofa, his hands on their shoulders. 'Hermione, my pet, Jackie my pet, we can't allow this, you must come and mix, everyone at my parties must mix – ' and they're up and away, he pats each on the buttocks as they scurry off. He shakes a reproving finger at Lydia. 'My dear, you're monopolizing him and his admirers await.'

'We were building up a meaningful relationship,' I say, finishing off my martini.

'Nay, lad, we'll have none of those dirty southern goings-on here,' he says, mimicking a Yorkshire accent rather well. 'This is a decent household, I'll have you know.' He looks at my glass censoriously. 'Nay, that's enough of that stuff now. There's champagne.'

'Let him have what he likes,' Lydia says, getting up in one movement. She squeezes my hand, kisses me lightly on the cheek, and walks quickly away.

'She's a lovely mover,' Peter says. 'She likes you, Tim. Isn't like that with everybody. My word, no.' We're moving along to the buffet now, his hand on my arm in a light but surprisingly firm grasp and somehow or other we're moving towards two chairs in another room with laden plates. 'She shows it when she doesn't like people. She read PPE at Oxford, you know.' There's now a bottle of champagne on the table and three glasses. 'She thought of going into the Diplomatic Service once. Lucky she didn't I always tell her, otherwise we'd have had World War Three long since.'

'And we might have won,' I say. He pours the champagne: the glasses are narrow, as they should be. The champagne is marvellous, hovering on the brink of sweetness, as full-bodied as it's possible for a champagne to be.

'You like it?' He's watching my face. I realize that he never relaxes, he's always watching everyone's reactions.

'Very much. It's not too damned dry. Tastes like the champagne the French keep for themselves.'

He looks pleased with me, actively pleased, as if he'd like to give me a pat on the head or a bag of sweets for being a good clever boy.

The young blonde shimmers up: we rise. He kisses her on both cheeks. 'When you're away, every minute seems a year, my sweet. This is my friend, Tim Harnsforth, the famous writer. Anna Redruth.'

She holds out a small apparently boneless hand. She has large surprisingly shrewd brown eyes which I can see entering an instantaneous judgement and filing it away for future reference. 'I was in a TV play of yours once. *All Sorts of Messages.*'

'Of course. I remember you.'

'I was only on for a second. A face in the crowd.'

We sit and she absentmindedly eats from Peter's plate. He looks at her indulgently. 'She really is very talented, Tim.'

'I believe you,' I say, eating a slice of guinea fowl. I look around. The furniture is solid but commonplace, the walls plain white, there's nothing to distract attention from the pictures. He follows my glance.

'You really must come some day and look round at your leisure.'

'I like your pictures,' I said.

'I'm delighted. You don't like abstracts, do you? Neither do I. Even when they're good – I have a couple of Albert Irvins which you might like – what have you got? Wallpaper and curtain designs.'

He refills my glass and the evening takes off and from now on it's not so much a question of a blackout but a montage – the long corridors and empty squares of Chirico; the austerity of Wyeth; the matchstick figures of Lowry; a Vernet battle scene I'd not seen before; dancing with Lydia; dancing with Anna; briefly arguing with a tall thin grey-haired director called Neil Canvey about Wyeth and about Dennis Potter; and then it steadies down.

Neil Canvey has a slim tall red-haired girl with him half his age; he speaks quite plainly most of the time but then mumbles and I catch her name as Tracy Mumble-Mumble. She has large green eyes which focus relentlessly on Canvey all the time; he looks at her with a proprietorial pleasure. His face in fact is gaunt and disapproving and would be best suited for a Calvinist hellfire-and-damnation preacher of the old school; but as far as it can convey pleasure it does so when he looks at her.

'Peter has no taste at all,' Canvey says. '*None at all*. He chooses by name. Ah, all this stuff is pleasant enough but the difference between this and the real stuff – and there is some around, he's hedging his bets – is the difference between – ' He looks around him for words as if they were actually in the air in front of him, and then grabs a handful – 'well, if you don't mind me saying so, like the difference between your plays and Dennis Potter's. Or David Mercer's.'

I grin. 'I don't mind your saying so, as long as the difference is to their disadvantage.'

'Your arrogance is ill-founded,' he snaps.

I look at him and begin to laugh. And then I'm dancing with Lydia again; she has effortlessly extricated me from Neil Canvey and Tracy Mumble-Mumble and this dance, for a wonder, is a waltz and we're dancing cheek to cheek.

She kisses me on the mouth lightly. 'Are you married?'

'Of course I'm married.'

'How many children do you have?'

'Three by the present one. A son and two daughters. And

I've a son by my first marriage.'

'I have two boys. They're at prep school. Or rather generally are.'

'They're boarders?' I'm beginning to have an erection but am also beginning to feel rather sleepy.

'What else? The good old English middle-class tradition. Won't you with yours?'

'My wife doesn't hold with it.'

'She's not here this evening, I see.'

'She isn't terribly keen on society.'

'You mean society with a capital s, or society generally?'

'Both. So we've come to a working arrangement. Buckingham Palace garden parties or the Lord Mayor's Dinner – OK. Anything else – ' I grimace. It's too tiresome to explain.

'She's very foolish. Attractive men who go to parties by themselves are likely to be stolen. London is full of predatory ladies.'

'Maybe she doesn't think anyone will want to steal me.'

'Stop fishing for compliments.' She rubs against my groin and I forget that I'm sleepy.

And then I'm sitting at a table in another room and Tracy Mumble-Mumble has introduced a short man with a ginger beard as her brother, Nat, and I somehow gather that Nat's in public relations and despises it. He also appears to despise me.

'You're absolutely cynical,' he is saying, stabbing the air with a short fat manicured forefinger. 'My God, when I was at Oxford I used to worship you. I heard you speak at a CND meeting once. You had ideals then, and a good loud strong voice...'

I don't know what I'm saying to him. All the faces seem a long way away. And now it's past midnight and there's a long day ahead of me tomorrow even though it is a Saturday, because I've got to make up for the working time lost today. And now I see Neil Canvey coming towards me and the last thing I want to do is to talk to him. So I stand suddenly. 'I have to go. Lovely meeting you'.

And then – I can find in my memory no trace of any intervening period – I'm sitting beside Lydia in a white Triumph Stag with the top down and she's wearing a pale grey suede jacket and a blue Hermes headscarf and the night air's cold on my face and Haverstock Hill with its trees and buildings as clean as dolls' houses is soon Camden Town and the kebab and hamburger joints and discos and the pubs with crowds outside and police cars with flashing blue lights and bodies on the pavement and the urban wasteland, the loneliness approaching Waterloo and Waterloo itself.

'Jules' Bar at six,' Lydia says kissing me.

'Jules' Bar at six.' The Stag sidles off – she's a casual and smooth driver – and I walk to the Boxley platform. I'm quite sober now and don't really want to go home but there's nowhere else for me to go.

Five

Now it's a month after my first meeting with Lydia and we're in Jules's Bar on Jermyn Street at about six o'clock at the beginning of October. This was where we generally began the evening, and I grew very fond of the place. There's a long bar, there are good cocktails, it's small enough not to feel hemmed in. There's always somewhere to sit, it's never too crowded but never empty either. The décor is quiet, opulent without making a fuss about it; I suppose exactly what one would expect from a cocktail bar in Jermyn Street.

It's very good being here with Lydia, just what I need. She has on a low-cut scarlet silk blouse this evening, quite opaque but with no bra, and tight blue slacks and high black boots. I've finished my novel and for a while there's nothing more I can do about it. I'm not displaced any longer since I'm with an attractive woman in a pleasant place – and beginning my second Screwdriver.

'You're looking very well,' Lydia says. 'You really are. Better than when we first met.'

'It's you I have to thank for it. Do you remember in *Black Lamb and Grey Falcon* when Rebecca West tells how the Empress Elizabeth deliberately brought the actress Catherine Schratt into Franz Joseph's life? She was a very pretty sunny-natured girl, and Rebecca West says something like this: she brought her into his life as one would bring a vase of flowers into a dreary room to brighten it. That's how I feel about you.'

Her eyes moisten. She puts her hand on mine. 'Why, that's the nicest thing I ever had said to me. Particularly now. Sodding Peter is living in Miss Redruth's pocket. He's never been like this before. Must be the male menopause.'

'I thought you had — an understanding.'

She laughs. 'Oh yes. The famous understanding. One drifts into it. But he always seems an affair ahead of me. I'm not so sure that I'm an affair sort of person. I like to take things easy. Do you have an understanding with your wife?'

'Not exactly.' I'm nearly about to tell her everything, then am overcome by a feeling of shame and humiliation. 'She's what they call a homebody. Her face turns black with rage whenever she gets an invitation — the sort of invitation any normal woman would give her right arm for.'

'Odd. I suppose she's insecure.'

'No reason why she should be. She's nice-looking, she's a qualified librarian, we have three marvellous children — '

'You might be rather overpowering. Too rich for her blood, as the Americans say.'

'Am I too overpowering for you?'

'My dear, after Peter you're a rest-cure. He never stops wheeling and dealing, making friends and influencing people. You're as easy as an old shoe.'

I smile. 'My God, I'd never thought of myself quite like that before.'

'Perhaps you don't know yourself. You were rather a surprise to me. You're a bogeyman to the lefties, you know. They tell their kids that if they're not good and don't eat up their muesli, Tim Harnforth will get them.'

'Like Jimmy Knocker. Jimmy Knocker's very tall and thin and he makes naughty little boys into dripping. Oh, I had a tough upbringing.'

She shakes her head. 'No, you were spoilt. You always have been. You're so damned pleased with yourself, yet such a baby.' To my surprise I feel her hand under the table on my knee, moving upwards. 'Mummy's boy. You're Mummy's boy.'

Normally this is not the sort of description which a man cares to be applied to him, but I have a sense of *déjà vu* which doesn't, as it usually does, carry with it foreboding and trepidation. And I don't try to remember where I was before, I accept the mystery with gratitude.

'That's fair enough,' I say to Lydia. 'Right from the start my mother assured me that I was handsome, irresistibly charming, and a genius.'

'Is she still alive?'

'She died in a road accident in 1950.'

'I'm sorry. I shouldn't have asked.'

'Why ever not? I like to think of her. I still miss her. That's my one regret: she never saw my children, she never saw my first novel, she never saw me become what she'd always dreamed of me becoming.'

'What about your father?'

'Oh, he's still very much alive. Seventy-nine and as fit as a fiddle. He married again in 1951. A nice woman, a widow a few years younger than himself.'

'Did you resent it?'

'Good God, no.'

This is our fifth meeting. It's the meeting at which she asked me the sort of personal questions which most women ask much sooner. She really is a cool customer – cool not cold, completely reasonable, very much self-contained. It's a refreshment after Val, and whilst I'm with her there's no sense of displacement. She hates scenes and fuss just as, I'm sure, she hates dirt and disorder. But mixed in with all this there's poetry, not only in her physical presence but in her calmness and control, her meticulous elegance. I can't imagine her raising her voice. So far there have been only kisses, on meeting and parting and at odd moments in the car. I tell myself that it isn't civilized to come to conclusions too quickly, that, as with all the others, once I've had my curiosity about her body fully gratified, the affair will quickly end. And these are the reasons why I don't invite her to the flat in Monkman Street, why I haven't told her about it. But are they the real reasons?

Yes, I'm happy. There's the feeling, too, that I'm getting my own back on Val. It's not a feeling I'm proud of, but it's natural enough. I haven't told Val about us, but sometimes I have a vindictive desire to do so. But then I reflect that she's not really having it all her own way, for though at home I live with constant frustration, and my increasing resentment is poisoning me, now at least I have Lydia to think about. She's there as an ally, I have someone on my side. Yes, it does add up to happiness. But what I push to the back of my mind is that there's a deep flaw in this happiness, that something is about to go badly wrong.

There is something else: Bresson's *Lancelot du Lac*. This is here too. I mean that it's in the back of my mind all the time, just as *Les Enfants du Paradis* is, it is a collection of pictures which seem to say something especially for me. *Lancelot du Lac* is a film which I didn't enjoy but couldn't take my eyes away from. I don't think that the script follows the traditional story. The characters quarrel all the time, as I suppose they did in the thirteenth century. It's in love with death really. It ends with a great battle and a pile of horses and bodies, some still twitching. The fights are as if in a dream – bitterly real and salty with sweat and the smell of horses and leather and grass and blood and earth, but in slow motion. This was how it would be, since the armour and equipment weighed so much.

I've often wondered why this film means so much to me, because basically I found it boring but not depressing. It's savage and sombre but not lugubrious. Perhaps sometimes I miss the War. At any rate, I found myself missing the War then, but I didn't miss letting off with a Sten gun in the general direction of the enemy, which is just about all that I ever did. Nor did I miss being frightened and intolerably confused. What I miss, what I still miss, is the feeling of living for a purpose outside oneself. At this time in Jules's Bar with Lydia among the pictures from *Lancelot du Lac* is a positive craving for something large and disastrous to happen, but something which won't involve me being hurt. One can't long for a war any more for the obvious reason that it would mean mass annihilation.

This is what is in my mind at that time. I've never been so unhappy. Even when I'm with Lydia there's the feeling of something being not quite right, of her being the wrong person for me. But this is masked by the fact that in a quiet way we get through a great deal of alcohol when we go out together. And most evenings when I'm at home I manage to put away half a bottle of Scotch – very slowly, sip, sip, sip, and I'm never drunk but never in the evenings quite sober. The Scotch takes the edge off things, and there's Vanessa and Penelope always, that continuing physical affection. Simon is more self-contained, Simon is a boy, conditioned since school age to believe that it's unmanly to show physical affection. I love him but not in the same way as Penelope and Vanessa who hug and kiss spontaneously, who sit on my knee, who take my hands: and they're so pretty, so unselfconsciously and vividly feminine, that when they're there and when the Scotch takes the edge off things, I can most of the time keep the worst of the bitterness at bay. I can pretend that Val's a sister or a housekeeper, I can not be absolutely overcome by the sense of displacement.

And the book is finished. That's one of the strangest things which ever happened to me. It's about Michael Jenkins, a middle-aged man with a grown-up family, running a toy factory very successfully, whose marriage has for some twenty years been increasingly a matter of habit. He isn't me; he is in fact several people whom I know. And, just as he's reached the stage where he's about to let sex slip away – his wife being the sort who acquiesces resignedly instead of co-operating joyously – he meets a woman in her forties with three children still at school, and then what happens is stated in the title *Praise to the Evening*: there is love again, existence is an ecstatic simpleton, there are hands encountering across the table, there are snatched kisses and they almost seem enough, there are little secret gifts, there are even poems. And then a marvellous untidy frenzy in the back of his Jaguar and now she is his mistress, he's having an affair, he is more alive than ever before and his small world, so prosperous and secure and peaceful, is dangerous, exciting, charged with the threat of violence. And he's understanding more, he's transformed, women in particular look at him in a different way. He has changed his life, he has broken free.

And then he wants his home life no more, it weighs him down. It's all too sensible and ordered – bridge, golf, his model collection, the Rifle Club, now and again a day at the races, select guests for dinner and parties which never become rowdy. There's no surprises, no poetry. He only wants Antonia. He wants to have the minimum of possessions, he wants to centre his life upon Antonia.

In the end she goes away. She needn't go away: to cut a long story short, she persuades her husband to take a job in another part of the country. She has her children. And perhaps she knows that the house, the model collection, his whole way of life aren't something which Michael can leave behind. But then one Saturday afternoon in summer, no one else in the house, his wife away at the craft market, the house clean and tidy and empty, he realizes that Antonia is gone. Emptiness, all is empty, this is the holiday season and most of the houses on the avenue are empty and the cypresses look as if cut out of metal and there is no breeze and, in this cul-de-sac, no sound of traffic. There's nowhere he wants to go and nothing he wants to look at on the TV and nothing he wants to read and he doesn't want to get drunk and he doesn't want to do any gardening and the garden in any case is in perfect order. So he goes into the gunroom to clean his guns, but they're already clean. And then he goes to the attic, moves the old bed there, takes out his bunch of keys, and turns a key in the floor, lifting out the .38 Black Hawk Magnum Ruger. He has a box of slugs in his pocket.

He sits on the bed and loads the gun. The attic is large and was used by his sons for their model railway and model slot racing layouts, but the layouts have disappeared long since. There's only an old Scalextrix control unit and a broken Scalextrix Le Mans Bentley. He picks it up, dimly remembering that that series was never really satisfactory. There was an Alfa Romeo too, if his memory served him, but the cars were really too big to take corners at any speed. He did bring his own firm's slot racers home to test once, but they'd given up making them some ten years ago: there was too much hassle for too little profit.

He puts the Bentley down very gently and takes up the gun, his favourite of all his guns, wondering as he takes it up who the hell buys all the millions of handguns which must be made all over the world. The attic is very bare and very quiet and very well-lit. Antonia went away a week ago: they couldn't make love for one more time because it was the wrong day of the month and in any case they only had an hour together. She had to fight hard not to cry because it would look strange if she came back home in tears. But it was best that she should go for the sake of the children, she had said, though God knows the little sods would never thank her. Will you be all right, Michael? Don't do anything foolish. That's the way it is in this world: if you love anyone, they die or they go away.

And now there is nothing real and nothing alive and he can't sleep and there is nothing that he wants. It's not so bad when he's at the factory, but the business is going smoothly now, they haven't made the mistakes others have made, and his eldest son has new ideas and it's about time that he took a back seat. There's no one to explain all this to: he has a lot of friends but in the year that he's been in love with Antonia he's grown used to a different kind of friendship, a warmer affection, a stronger taste. There has been danger too, a certain feeling of guilt, he's been able to swagger a little. Now he's a man in his mid-fifties, a solid citizen, a respected figure in the community, and he doesn't know who he is or what the point of his existence is.

He lays the barrel of the gun against his cheek: he had expected it to be cold but it's warm. He releases the safety-catch and brings up the gun to his temple. Then he shivers convulsively, puts it down, takes off the safety-catch, unloads it, and puts it away again. He walks slowly out of the attic, the uncarpeted floorboards creaking under his feet.

This isn't the part which is prophetic: I've never even for one moment contemplated suicide or, come to that, owned a gun. What is prophetic is the fact that Michael had his life transformed by love. I'm proud now of having finished *Praise to the Evening* when I promised. It wasn't like this story to write. For I know far less about Tim Harnforth than I do about Michael Jenkins. I haven't ever really met Tim Harnforth, I merely live with him. I've met Michael Jenkins a hundred times. You know where you are with Michael, he's relatively predictable. And Michael has an interesting job, Michael makes things, physical objects. He is, so to speak, both artist and man of action. Tim Harnforth has his study at home and his office in a room on the ground floor of Number Twenty-One Main Street, Boxley, with a barber's shop at the front and the barber's flat on the first floor. He goes there every day from Monday to Friday – since Vivien, except Thursday – from nine to six and makes black marks on white paper. There can be involvements in TV, in films, in journalism, in radio, there can be script conferences and lunches and dinners and cocktail parties, there can be people who have power over him or who can do him a favour, there can be a certain amount of power politics entailed, but eventually he ends up alone making black marks on white paper.

And Michael has genuine relationships, real feelings. If he loves or hates – not that he's any great hand at hating – he isn't asking himself all the time what use he can make of this, he isn't looking for words to describe it. I've told you about Tim Harnforth's time of displacement. Fair enough:

this is what he felt. (I express it in this way because I'm trying to distance myself from him.) But at his worst, when he was really suffering – as he had good reason to – he was at bottom rather pleased at what had happened to him. It was a new experience and it was valuable. Michael is very different. He suffers, he's entirely taken over by suffering, a rabbit screaming in a gin-trap.

There's the difference. What's astounding is the likeness between us in the matter of happiness. How did I know so authentically before I met Vivien that a middle-aged man could love a middle-aged woman and be loved by her and they both would be completely fulfilled? I wasn't writing from experience. For I had lived for some twenty years with a woman and hadn't truly loved her or been loved by her, and had had a hundred women and not loved them. (Though some of them may, for all I know, have loved me.)

True, I had been very near to loving Gillian. But I was too young to appreciate all that she gave me. And I thought that I loved Shirley, my first wife, for a while, but then I realized overnight that I didn't when she left me for Jack Cessnock. I love as the pagans love: I love those who love me. And I thought that I loved Val. And I'd cobbled up some sort of arrangement with her based on sex and the children, but I had when I wrote that last chapter, long since come to terms with the fact that she didn't love me.

So here I am, roughly five years ago, in October driving along in Hertfordshire in the silver Bug convertible which I had then. It is Indian-summer weather and I have the top down and I feel happy in an uncomplicated almost naïve sort of way. The countryside is curiously deserted. In its way it's richer and lusher even than Surrey, rentier's country, stockbroker's country, gentleman farmer's country, weekend cottage country, country where they still dress for dinner and never worry about money. It isn't, of course, tourist country and doesn't encourage tourists. It's intensely private; indeed, when I occasionally pass through a village, I have a feeling of active hostility. The people who live here, I feel, don't like anyone from outside very much: they might break into the peculiar English bourgeois dream of being ladies and gentlemen. I'm quite happy thinking about this, not in a political sort of way and not bothering overmuch about the morality of it, but simply ruminating about it professionally. There is power here, power which doesn't have the self-confidence which it once had, power which has been tainted by a creeping liberalism, but which still can, however discreetly and smoothly, enforce its wishes, which still can reach out and touch even me. The family who once owned my publishers live somewhere near Hoddesdon; I've never met any of them but remember hearing talk of a huge manor house and home farm and reflect that I have probably paid for at least a hundred crates of Bollinger and a couple of Jersey cows.

I'm free and, as always, given half a chance, certain that something wonderful may happen. What, I'm not quite sure. I'm not expecting it to be connected with sex. If I want sex, then there is Lydia; but I can't, of course, quite connect sex with Lydia. There should be a connection, we know one another well enough by now, we like one another well enough, I don't think that she's the platonic type, the flat in Monkman Street is available: what's holding me back?

I'm thinking about this with such intensity that I miss the sign to Brotton Manor; I'm already in the long narrow main street of Brotton itself, a not particularly appealing town — an overgrown village rather than a town, mostly in red brick, with a few concrete fronts. I stop the car and look behind me and realize that it's a one-way street and that I can only go forward. Half an hour later after travelling round a featureless industrial estate, a wasteland of huge deserted concrete buildings and long roads leading to other long roads and no signs which are of any help, I find myself in the dual carriageway again then into the main street again. It's half-past three on a Saturday afternoon and most of the shops seem to be open, but there seem to be few people around. I've often noticed this in areas near London:

the life seems to have gone out of them. Even Boxley has more vitality, at weekends it's full, there's life going on with all its marvellous untidiness, people are mixing, there's even a sense of community, people recognize each other, they're part of a greater whole. I have a feeling of a town which has lost its will to live; and then I'm taking the narrow road to the left and passing by old stone houses, then through woodland, then down a long drive, the grass on the verges rather unkempt, and stopping at the front of Brotton Manor, a huge building in mellow red brick in the traditional E-shape layout with the centre horizontal, a large entrance porch. It is indeed exuberantly Elizabethan with oriel windows and corkscrew-shaped chimneys – too Elizabethan to be authentic. But it's great fun and by the time I've found the car park I find my spirits rising yet higher.

The truth is that I enjoy public speaking, which I do very well. And I like being made a fuss of; not that I'm absolutely certain of that this weekend. In fact I'm rather surprised at being asked. My host is the Radical Association, a rather old-fashioned society, liberal and pacifist rather than left-wing, which has been prospering quietly since the 1920s. I reflect as I go into a large oak-panelled room with ENQUIRIES tacked above the door that they're probably so old-fashioned that they don't politicize absolutely everything, that perhaps they actually like to hear from people whose views differ from theirs.

Inside a harassed-looking man in his sixties, tall and stooping, who really does look as if his shabby tweeds have literally been flung on, and the knot of whose bright red tie is edging towards his left ear, is talking to a large plump cheerful woman in her forties. There's a pile of forms and letters and cheques and an open cash-box on the long trestle table in front of them. There's half-a-dozen folding wooden slatted chairs dotted about the room, and a large grey steel filing-cabinet, a bookcase mostly containing directories, and a small office desk in beech with a shrouded typewriter on it and a swivelling typist's chair.

'Ah, Mr Harnforth,' the harassed-looking man said. 'I recognize you from your photo. My name's Basil Gregg – we've been in touch of course.' He held out a bony hand.

'Delighted to meet you.' I give him my most sincere smile.

'And this is Bridget Ormagh, my right-hand woman. She's a great fan of yours, too.'

I shake Bridget Ormagh's hand. She has an Indian print dress and a large but agreeable bosom. 'I'm delighted to meet you too, Mrs Ormagh.'

'I'm a great admirer of yours, you know.' She smiles. Her teeth are very good.

'As indeed many of us are,' Basil Gregg says. 'There's a plan of the rooms in what we jocularly term the Great Hall, from where you've come in. And tea's being brewed now. Should you require something stronger, the bar's open at half-past five.' The last remark is made rather disapprovingly.

Actually, I think I'll have a wash and freshen up, and then look through my notes. I'll see you later.'

'I'll look forward to your talk. Mind – ' he shakes his finger at me – 'you must promise to be provocative. We believe in speaking out at the Radical Association. We'll positively enjoy it if we disagree with you.'

'I appreciate that. That's why I value the invitation.' I smile my way out and find my way to my bedroom, a small room obviously once part of a larger room, with white painted walls, one in hardboard, a divan bed, a white wardrobe, a small oak desk, a small armchair, a washbasin, and a small dressing-table. It's at the back of the house and there's a view of some very pleasant parkland. There's an old-fashioned radiator, big and bloated, which is already clanking and hissing: it's far from being a luxurious room, but at least I won't be cold. I take off my jacket and shirt and cravat, take out my towel and soapbag and wash my face and hands. I run the electric shaver over my face then put on some Braggi with a lavish hand. I put on my shirt and cravat again, take out my notes and pour a generous measure of Black and White into my tooth-glass.

I can't be got at, I'm a free man, there's nothing to worry about, not even a deadline, *Praise to the Evening* is nearly ready for the printer. What I have ahead of me – but not until tomorrow morning – is to speak for three-quarters of an hour and answer questions for three-quarters of an hour, which is hard work, but child's play compared with the effort entailed even in writing the briefest piece. And I'll meet new people, I'll add to my stock of material almost without knowing it.

I begin to think, not in a very urgent way, about what slant I'll give my talk tomorrow and remember what I said to Lydia at Jules' Bar. I sip the whisky and scribble in my notebook: JOKES: *Asimov pianist, Maternity ward* – then can't remember a third, or at least not one which isn't dirty. The two I've put down are merely mildly improper; the Radical Association will feel itself very broad-minded indeed to laugh at them. The whisky warms my stomach gently; the effect is all the more immediate because it's the first of the day. I may be an idiot, but I honestly never drink and drive. And I slept late this morning and had time for no more than a cup of tea. This is a moment of happiness, because no one can get at me and, until I leave this room, the pressure's off. I'll remember a third joke if I stop trying to remember.

I make a few more notes and then am overcome by a feeling of desolation. I'm mindful that I have to watch the whisky. It's little temptation during the working day, but I'm beginning to feel a little frightened. For more and more often I find myself sitting up late in my study drinking. It's in the blood on the Irish side: more than one of my relations have died of drink. I remember my Uncle Michael, who never married and who died at the age of forty, with his bloated red face, bloodshot eyes, shuffling walk and trembling hands. He was a carpenter in a small way but never built the business up as he could have done. He worked only to buy himself drink – Bushmill's Irish whisky as I remember, with Tetley's bitter as a chaser. The first two fingers on the big square hands – hands like mine, Irish navvy's hands – were always stained bright yellow by the Woodbines which he chain-smoked. Strangely enough – I remember this now – his hands never trembled when he was working.

My mother once told me that in her opinion he'd started drinking because he felt guilty about not being killed in the Great War like his brother Desmond, but since he was only twelve when the war began I think this extremely unlikely. My Uncle Michael wasn't a person who felt guilty even when he had every reason to be. A boy of sixteen in 1918 wasn't, as his counterpart in 1914 would have been, frightened that the war would end before he got a chance to be in it. He was frightened that it wouldn't end, that he'd be killed or horribly mutilated. My Uncle Michael was a sot, but he was no fool. I can only presume that on some occasion when the drink had brought the play-actor in him to the surface, but he hadn't had enough to rob him of coherent speech, he'd wanted to tell my mother what a noble fellow he was. I don't think that my mother was taken in, but perhaps she wanted him to have some shadow of an excuse for being the pitiable wreck that he was.

I refill my glass, the depression gone. I shall use all this. I haven't used any of my relations in my talks before. Come to that, this will be the first time I've talked about my mother. I remember her now, small, plump, black-haired, singing 'Just a Song at Twilight'. It's growing dark and the sky has a reddish tinge. We're in the house where I lived as a child. We only have an immediate view of a small backyard with what used to be an outside WC but is now a toolshed, and a narrow alleyway backing on to another identical terrace. But if one were to continue up the steeply sloping street at the front, it ends in a footpath which leads to Casterley Moor. There's a blazing coal fire and my mother's sitting by it, quite happily singing in an untrained but sweet contralto. With all her faults, she made a vocation of happiness.

But the song doesn't make me happy. She's putting all

that she's got into it, all her enormous emotional energy is directed upon me. I can't think how old I was; but my sisters weren't there, so presumably they were on their way home from school, and as I wasn't at school I must have been about four. 'Just a song at twilight, when the lights are low, And the flickering shadows Softly come and go ...' I sing the song softly to myself and am surprised to find the tears start to flow. I'm not crying just because my mother's dead now, I'm not crying because once there was one person who was entirely upon my side and now there's no one. That's part of it, true; and the whisky helps. But I'm crying because of that damned song. It's so lost, so hopeless, it makes me feel trapped. And now I have a nightmare vision of how I might have been living in Yorkshire somewhere; but not Casterley, some dingy little town in South Yorkshire where the only action is in the pubs and clubs and it's a day's march to open country and all the phone boxes and schools are vandalized and the spoil heaps dominate the drab little houses. And the song puts me there, alone, unknown, living in digs, holding down some lousy routine job, different from the rest in the town, seen partly as a figure of fun, partly as someone superior, someone who reads more than is good for him or any human being, someone who has all sorts of odd ideas, particularly after he's had a few pints. That's the only time he's halfway human, like. Doesn't see you, otherwise. Head in t'bloody clouds. Nay, I don't know where he came from. But I tell you what it is, you've always that funny feeling that he's laughing at you. Thinks he's bloody superior. He hasn't got two halfpennies to rub together, not that it seems to bother him. I tell you what gets on my wick: the way he'll look right through you. Well-spoken? He's never at a loss for a word, but I wouldn't call him well-spoken exactly. Buggered if I know what to call it. Queer? Oh aye, I know what you mean. Not that way. But the way you mean he's as queer as Dick's hatband. Has he ever been wed? He has that look. If he has been, he doesn't let on ... *But still to us at twilight comes Love's old song – Comes love's old sweet song* . . .

And my tears are flowing back in Casterley. 'Don't go on, Mummy,' I'm entreating her, 'it's too sad.' Which makes her put more and more emotion into it. She is for the moment in her imagination holding a crowded hall by the magic of her voice. And now she'll either sing another Victorian ballad, 'The Drunkard's Daughter', which makes me weep even more copiously, or 'The Irish Rebel's Song', or 'The Wearing of the Green' or, very occasionally, 'Amazing Grace', which I really enjoy.

And now I'm back at Brotton Manor refilling my glass and noting it all down: *More re songs and Casterley – true artist* . . . I'm going to use part of my past. I'm going to say that I still miss her. Then I think of something else. My grandmother Cloneen had two sons, Matthew and Gerard, who died at two and four of epidemic enteritis. Then her daughter Mildred died of typhoid at the age of fifteen. My grandmother wouldn't eat, wouldn't drink, wouldn't speak. She was like a zombie. Mildred had made a great pet of her four-year-old sister Sarah, who was always crawling into her bed for cuddles and comfort, as children of that age do. They had tried to keep Sarah away from Mildred, but she must have got into her room. A week after Mildred died, Sarah died. And then my grandmother wept. The doctor said that if she hadn't wept she'd have gone mad.

And now I'm weeping and I can't stop it, it's frightening me. Because I remember my grandparents' house in Inkerman Terrace opposite St Bridget's where my grandfather was verger. It always smelled of roast beef and tapers. I've used that house, I've used my grandparents, but I've never used the story of Mildred and Sarah. I don't know why, except that it didn't fit. I haven't thought about Mildred and Sarah for a long time and now that I have, I'm still crying. I cry to soldiers marching to a band, I find my eyes moistening when I know that I've written really well, I cry sometimes at certain poems:

Out of the rolling ocean the crowd came a drop gently to me,
Whispering I love you, before long I die,
I have travelled a long way merely to look upon you, to touch you,
For I could not die till I once looked on you,
For I feared I might afterwards lose you.

And now I'm still weeping. It's so perfect, the beat is so powerful, the emotion is absolutely pure, there is no artifice, it's a miracle, it surges forward and outward – it's there at Brotton Manor and it's here in another now, no more real, no less real, than it was at Brotton Manor. And it's overwhelmed me because of its perfection. Before Trafalgar Nelson showed his captains his battle plan and they all wept, not because they were frightened of dying, but because it was so perfect.

And now over four years later in my office at Broxley near the town centre, sitting in an old leather buttoned wing chair, a stiff-backed exercise book in my lap, I know how they felt. I know now and I knew then that what is important about my situation is not only that I can weep about the death of these two children all those years ago, but that Whitman makes me weep too. It's a different weeping. I mourn for the children and I mourn for those who loved them. Nothing ever dies, it's all going on. There's no mourning in the Whitman poem. It isn't sad, though there isn't a happy ending. It's beyond sadness and beyond happiness, it is there as the rolling ocean is there.

I'm back now at Brotton Manor drying my eyes. I put the notebook down, take off my jacket and shirt and scarf and wash my face. After I've dried it I put on some more Braggi cologne; the musky but peppery smell brings a note of festivity to the bare little room. I'm not drunk, but I've got through a third of the bottle of whisky and, since my talk isn't until tomorrow, I'm well aware that I'm going to get drunk. The bar, in a not very large oak-panelled room off

95

the main hall, is an austere affair with a blue formica
counter and a rather grim-faced middle-aged man in a
white jacket behind it. There doesn't seem to be any ice.
There are tables and only the ubiquitous slatted wood
folding chairs round the room; on the whole the impression
is that whoever is in authority at Brotton Manor doesn't
very much approve of drinking. There are about twenty
people there, mostly middle-aged, mostly – at a quick
glance at least – tweedy, earnest and middle-class. Then I
see Cedric Easington enter the room in a green corduroy
suit, green suede casuals and a pink cashmere sweater. He
rushes towards me.

'Tim, my dear!' He embraces me briefly, laying his cheek
against mine lightly as actors do. 'It's been a long time. Far
too long. We never see you at World Writers these days.'

'I must start coming again. How are you, anyway?'

'Thriving, as far as anyone in British theatre can be said
to thrive – ' His large brown eyes looked at me shrewdly.
'And you're well? Really, really well? And wife? And the
bambinos?'

Cedric's face is tanned winter and summer and has a
curious square dignity which somehow doesn't go with the
rest of him. Only the full mouth and the lively eyes one feels
are rightfully his.

'Everyone is really, really well,' I say lightly. 'Won't you
have a drink?'

'No, dear, on me. I'm much better at this sort of thing
than you. And it's double Scotch, on the rocks, as I remember.' All the time we're speaking he's making his way to the
bar. 'Oh, I'm not just a pretty face.' He glances behind him
as Tibor and Ruth Bachony, Glenda Farnham, Roddy and
June Glenthorn, and a black-haired woman in a red dress
enter the room. 'Our little party from World Writers.' He's
already at the bar and I'll swear that before he's spoken, the
barman, with something approaching a smile, is already
lining up drinks on a tray. 'Organize some seats, dear Tim.'

There are greetings and handshakes and kisses; I know

all Cedric's party from meeting them at World Writers, except the black-haired woman in the red dress, who is introduced to me as Vivien Canvey.

And that's the first time I met Vivien. Looking at it from my office in Boxley now, four years after, I'm struck by the fact that I had absolutely no intimation that my life was going to change. Tim Harnforth before that meeting and Tim Harnforth now are almost two different persons. The only love I really had experienced then at its fullest was love for my children. My love for my father and mother and sisters and for my friends was genuine enough, but there was something missing. There was a coldness at the heart somewhere. I hadn't ever really loved a woman. I hadn't ever given myself. There'd been a certain amount of affection, but no more. I think that they all knew it. There would be moments with them all when they'd be speaking a different language and there'd be a certain sadness in their voices when they realized I hadn't understood that language. I think that when I met Val I was determined to love her properly, I was determined to give her all that I had to give. But perhaps then I was using the language of love imperfectly, I'd tried to learn it consciously, I'd learned the grammar and had a passable accent, but I hadn't mastered the idiom.

I didn't, of course, love Lydia. I liked her and was physically attracted to her. She was in my mind a good deal of the time at Brotton. But I was angry and hurt at my rejection by Val, the mother of my children. My motive for the relationship with Lydia was almost entirely my damaged self-esteem. But then – and it's literally only now in my office at Boxley that I've realized it – it was simply a case of history repeating itself. When Shirley left me my self-esteem was damaged. Val – and this is something I was grateful for at the time – helped to repair it. Plain straightforward animal desire would have been a better motive for marrying her. Friendship, a genuine friendship, and let the sex look after itself, would have been better still.

What surprises me now is how little I knew about myself, how little experience had taught me. Sex did look after itself when I was younger. It looked after itself even when I actually didn't like the woman. Just as I'd used Val so I hoped to use Lydia. But I was thirty-four when I met Val and fifty-two when I met Lydia. And when I met Val I was drinking only moderately and when I met Lydia my drinking was becoming an increasing problem, it wasn't fun any more.

I often wish that I hadn't been so drunk when first I met Vivien. It doesn't entirely spoil the memory: it's still something to hold on to. All that matters is that it happened. All that matters is that without me knowing it then my life abruptly lurched on to the right track. But if Vivien had been drunk too, that would have been the end of it, and I'm pretty sure that I would have lurched into disaster, the crackup to end all crackups.

I'm not yet pissed out of my mind but Brotton Manor has transformed itself since my arrival. It's warm and cosy, it's as if there were a roaring log-fire somewhere. I feel well-disposed towards the world. What Val has done to me ceases to have any relevance. I'm sure that I'm on the verge of being both witty and profound. I'm marching at the head of a brass band and all the wonderful people in the room are marching with me.

They are actually mostly middle-aged, tweedy if men, floral fabrics if women, with a sprinkling of young people in the usual uniform of blue denim or Indian print. They are actually rather quiet: our party is, without being rowdy, the noisiest, since we are all in our varying degrees, prima donnas.

Tibor and Ruth Bachony are oddly alike, both short with sleek black hair and round cheerful faces. But Tibor's face somehow or other is acquainted with power, has been in the world of action, and Ruth's face is tranquil, English bourgeois, certain that the trams will be running and there'll be no shooting in the streets. For all that, Tibor was born in

England and has lived all his life there and is profoundly and cynically apolitical and Ruth was born in the USA and is passionately anti-Communist. Glenda Farnham is rather a good novelist, small, quiet, fair-haired, with large blue eyes which always have a faintly surprised expression. Roddy Glenthorn is tall and thin, with a face which has an element of dash about it, an abstracted expression and a way of suddenly delivering remarks resoundingly beneath the belt; June is nearly as tall as him with a face which is angular, nervy, feminine, and somehow art deco. They'd make a rather good Elyot and Amanda for *Private Lives*. I don't know their ages but have a dim idea that all the men are in their late forties and all the women in their late thirties.

I ruminate on this fact rather muzzily: it seems to me enormously significant. I look at Vivien Canvey again, and more and more like what I see. I particularly like her skin, which is dazzlingly clear. She has an air of great vitality: she isn't boisterous, she isn't breezy, she's simply very much alive.

'I loved *The Weather on the Hills*,' she says to me. 'More even than your first.'

'I like it better than my first. No one else did. Except the public.'

'I expect the reviewers all had their knives out after the first.' She has a strong clear nicely-modulated voice with no local accent but no bourgeois gabbling or neighing either.

'You know how it is. They feel themselves to be king-makers. And what's the good of being a kingmaker if you can't unmake kings?'

All of this is remarkably coherent but I can feel the whisky at work. I'm aware that she's by far the most attractive woman in the room.

'I don't really know how it is personally,' Vivien says. 'I don't really get reviewed.'

'What do you write?'

'Children's books. Fashion books. Journalism.' She

smiles, showing very white teeth. 'I never refuse any offer.'

'I seem to remember your name. We must have met – '
The whisky now is beginning to pull out plugs from my
switchboard; not in any hurry, not making a fuss about it,
but slowly whistling between its teeth. I'm quite happy
about it in one part of my mind, but in another part I wish
things could have been different.

'You might have met my husband. He's a TV director.
Neil Canvey.' Her voice is quite neutral.

'That's it. We met briefly at Peter Rugeley's place.' I
remember dimly the tall thin grey-haired man and Tracy
Mumble-Mumble.

Cedric is beside us with a gin and tonic and a Scotch on
the rocks. 'Neil is a cunt, my dear Tim,' he says.

'Shush, Cedric,' Glenda Farnham says. 'You're shocking
everyone rigid.'

'Nonsense,' Cedric says. 'We'll shock them even more if
we're not completely outrageous in our behaviour.' He
looks at Vivien speculatively, then at me. 'Actually,' he says
to Vivien, 'You'd be very good for him and he'd be very
good for you.'

'They're the same sort of person, really,' June says. 'Not
really seventies. Almost 1914. They have bottom, wouldn't
you say?'

Vivien is laughing. She has a very pleasant laugh, full-
throated but not raucous. 'I might shock him,' she says.
'I'm a real lefty.'

'Not really,' Tibor says. Despite his having been born
and bred in England, his accent has a trace of the exotic, his
enunciation has an un-English precision. 'Vivien is an old-
fashioned social democrat.'

I'm drunk, but my mind's working very well. I'm aware
that if only I stop here, I'm going to be very happy. I'm
aware that I like her and she likes me and that I've never
met anyone like her before. I'm aware that we're in the right
company. I know everyone here quite well, have met them
at various parties, at meetings, at the BBC and PEN and

World Writers and clubs and Fleet Street pubs: the literary world in England is still a small one and still centred upon London. But I haven't been out and about in the literary world lately because more and more the life that its inhabitants lead has made me envious. Self-pity is creeping in: I put it aside.

And now it's all hazy. What does Vivien say next? I think that she mentions *The Weather on the Hills* again. I think that someone from the Radical Association, a large fat woman in a pink dress, is somehow or other drawn in and accusing me of being woefully misguided about Vietnam. And then we're at dinner and all I remember about the dinner is that it's lukewarm and Cedric's party has brought in some wine. 'High thinking and plain living,' Cedric says to me. Yes, I remember that. And I remember that Glenda's saying to me, very earnestly: 'Cedric is right, you know. Neil is a shit ...'

I taste the wine and it's very good. It's red wine, very soft. I don't know how I answer Glenda, though I'm conscious of liking her very much. I like Cedric and all of Cedric's party very much. Cedric, I think, is gay and good. Some gay people are very catty and need watching. They're destructive, they hate themselves for being gay and they hate the straights for not being gay. Cedric – I'm pretty sure I was thinking along these lines in a confused and genial way – is one of the old school, he gets on with his life in his own way, he just turns out a stream of good plays and minds his own business. I like Cedric and I like his wine and I'm sure that I'm telling him this and then I'm putting my hand very delicately on Vivien's cheek and it's unbelievably soft and smooth and I'm telling her that her skin is fantastically silky and clear and English and I can't tell whether her eyes are brown or green or grey but that they give me great pleasure and that they smile when her lips smile but sometimes they smile and her lips don't smile, they're speaking eyes. The strange thing is – and I'm sure about this – that at one point, though they're smiling, there's moisture in them.

The next thing we're in Roddy and June Glenthorn's bedroom, rather larger than mine, with two beds and the same white-distempered walls but with a rather large and handsome Victorian mahogany wardrobe and we're drinking whisky out of plastic cups. There are only two chairs, wooden kitchen chairs painted bright red for some reason; I'm sitting on a bed beside Vivien and in one sense I'm very pleased to be speaking to her and in another sense I'd be very happy simply to sit quietly with her. I know that Glenda is a good speaker and that she knows what she's talking about and that she always takes the trouble to be audible and I'm aware that I've told her at some point quite sincerely that I'm looking forward to her talk, but all that I really want to do is to sit here with Vivien, who smells very clean but not antiseptic and who has a strong musky perfume – vetiver somewhere I think – but who also smells quite simply like a woman. I'm not touching her. In any case, though my stomach is coping very well with the whisky and the wine, I know that I've reached a very delicate balance, that I feel not very far off being airborne, and any sort of action would spoil it, take me into the comic-postcard world of staggering and seeing double and being foolish instead of being, as I believe I am, supremely articulate and, so the whisky and the wine assure me, completely in control. I'm certain that I'm living as I should live, and with the people I should be with. For Vivien is not only with me, she's part of the group. And I realize how desperately lonely and unhappy I've been.

Then I'm in the main hall sitting next to Vivien. I don't quite know how I've got there. I'm not seeing double, I'm not hiccuping, I'm not about to be sick, but everything's out of focus except Vivien's face. I'm entranced by it, it's so much alive. Glenda is speaking now and whilst with one part of my mind I can appreciate that she's speaking very well, I don't really take it in. I'm remembering a line of poetry; I hunt around in my pocket and find an envelope and scribble it down. *Votre âme est un paysage choisi.* I hand it to Vivien and see her smile as she reads it.

'Oh, that's beautiful. I'll keep it.'

What did I say after that? I can't remember. I can with a great effort remember her saying something about sitting in the one-and-ninepennies. I can remember leaving the room, finding myself alone in a large cloakroom with some two dozen stalls and a dozen WCs, washing my hands, and feeling uncertain of finding my way back. There are tiled floors and a sense of desolation. Outside I meet a black labrador. I stroke him and he licks my hands. And now I'm beside Vivien again and I'm talking about the dog. Somehow it seems enormously significant that he should have licked my hands. And now there is nothing. It has all gone, Vivien tells me now that I kept on talking, modulating my voice to a piercing whisper when people in the audience started shushing me, and that among the things I said was, '*I'm going to make you come.*' And I say also, I'm quite certain, '*The waves are crashing on the beach and there's a high wind and we're not frightened. Let's watch the waves.*' I have these waves in my mind and I'm now seeing people dancing.

And then I'm in bed in my underpants, my clothes all over the floor and asleep immediately, and falling, falling, falling, remembering Rilke's lines, repeating them – *all have this falling sickness none withstands And yet there's One whose gentle hands This universal falling can't fall through.* And then it's daylight and I have a splitting head and queasy stomach and a dry mouth and I don't for a moment know where I am and I can't remember anything and there's a feeling of deep guilt and impending doom.

That's the worst part of it. I force myself out of bed, and moving very slowly, take the steps towards physical recovery – Alka-Seltzer, shower, shave, clean shirt and underwear and socks, a lot of cologne – and as I go into the dining-room I know that the headache and queasiness and dry mouth will disappear as soon as I've had bacon and eggs and toast and marmalade and a lot of tea. I shall in fact with extraordinary rapidity feel not simply not ill but positively well. What won't go away, what will poison the next twenty-four hours is the sense of deep guilt and impending doom.

Before I was pitchforked into displacement I was a stranger to both these feelings. I suppose that this was the result of a Catholic upbringing and a cheerful disposition. I can't ever remember feeling guilty about anything in my life, unless I count my desertion of my son Kevin. And now back in the present this begins to hurt me. It isn't fair: I did it for the best. Jack Cessnock behaved like a shit to me, but he wasn't himself a shit. He was perfectly willing to think of Kevin as his own child. Kevin was only one year old, too young to have become accustomed to me. For me to have visited him would have only confused him, wouldn't have given Jack a fair chance. And in any case I wasn't sure that I could bear to see Jack and Shirley together.

Shirley left me some twenty-six years ago. That marriage doesn't belong to this story. And yet, I realize now, it has everything to do with my story. Over four years after the time of displacement, I'm still sharing a home with a woman who, I have long since become convinced, has no love for me and perhaps really never had. But because I'm still guilty about Kevin, I can't leave any child of mine again. God knows I'm selfish, arrogant, spoiled; but Kevin told me once that when he was sixteen he used to cry himself to sleep because I was his father and I wasn't there. I won't ever again have any child of mine crying themselves to sleep because I'm not there, even if it breaks my heart.

It's now the morning after the night before at Brotton Manor. I'm finishing my breakfast and beginning to emerge from the physical effects of the hangover. It would make a better story and show me in a better light if that morning I'd been full of joy about Vivien. It should have been love at first sight. It would have been if I'd been sober. As it was, I had only the dimmest remembrance of her. I hadn't even got her phone number. I couldn't remember her name. I couldn't see anyone from the party the night before.

And now I'm in the conservatory adjacent to the dining-room, where there are actually a few comfortable chairs. I settle down in one with my notebook and begin to think out my talk. There's a tea-urn and glasses of orange squash on a trestle table near me and after a while I cut myself off from everything around me. I even begin to feel a kind of happiness.

There's the story about the theatrical agent, sitting in his palatial office one day saying, 'Don't phone me, I'll phone you,' when his secretary comes in to tell him that a man outside claims to have something to show him which is absolutely unique. 'I'll give him five minutes,' says the agent, and a man enters carrying a wooden box. 'Believe me, you've never seen anything like this before,' he says. He opens the wooden box to show a ten-inch pianist sitting at a little grand piano in flawless evening dress. He taps the box, and the ten-inch pianist plays the first five minutes of the Moonlight Sonata with absolute perfection. He taps the box again and the ten-inch pianist whirls round and takes a bow.

'My God, that *is* absolutely unique!' the agent says. 'I really haven't seen anything like that before. How did you acquire him?'

'I was on holiday in Ireland,' the man said, 'and I caught a leprechaun. He said I could have anything I wished if I let him go.'

'Anything?' the agent said. 'And you asked for a ten-inch pianist?'

'I made my wish perfectly explicit,' the man said. 'But unfortunately the leprechaun misheard.'

I wonder whether it's not a little too sophisticated for the Radical Association, which strikes me somehow as being rather straitlaced. But the main point of beginning with the story is to get them into a receptive mood and to remove from their minds the fear that they're going to be submitted to an hour of undiluted culture. After they've had their laugh, I'll say that the story has a message for each of us. Do any of us get what we want? No. We get a ten-inch pianist. I needn't say what we'd get if we asked for a ten-inch pianist. That, ladies and gentlemen, is one of the things the novel is about. It's about the sheer contrariness of life.

There's a good ten to fifteen minutes there. I go on to the story of the young woman who comes into the maternity ward one day to book a bed. The sister-in-charge takes down her particulars – name, address, age, married or unmarried, name of father. She isn't married. In due course she has her baby, goes away, and comes back the next year at the same time. She still isn't married. The name of the father is the same again. In due course she has her baby, goes away, and next year comes back at the same time. She still isn't married, and the name of the father is the same again. This is really too much: the sister's very indignant. 'My dear,' she says, 'what a selfish brute that man must be. Why won't he marry you? Is he married already?'

'Oh no,' the girl says. 'He's always asking me to marry him.'

'Well, why won't you marry him?'

'I don't like him.'

You well may laugh, ladies and gentlemen, but this story illustrates a profound truth about human nature. Sex is utterly unreasonable. It has nothing to do with common sense. It has nothing to do with friendship. It very often hasn't even anything to do with self-interest. It's terribly destructive. It virtually never has anything to do with the marriage of true minds. It hasn't very often much connection with love. It has been known for a man to be totally happy with a woman he doesn't go to bed with and totally unhappy with a woman he does go to bed with.

Now I've shut the world out. There are people all around me, but I don't see them. I haven't very much time – an hour and a half at the most, since I have to put in an appearance at Cedric's talk about writing for TV. There is no question of having anything to drink stronger than tea, because in any case I have to drive home. At this moment nothing matters except the talk. I'm already beginning to regret having had so much to drink the night before. But all this has to be put out of my mind. I think of what Cocteau said: the Muse ushers the artist into the empty room and points silently at the tightrope. That's what I need, and I'll say something about my mother. Ushers the artist into an empty room? It must be a huge room. But the image works. And I haven't used it much before.

All the time there's a sense of regret, a feeling that I've missed something, that I've lost my way in the dark dank woods and that someone has shown me a way out of the woods into the sunlight and I haven't followed them. The fact is that what happened the night before I scarcely remember at all. I reconstruct most of it from what Vivien told me.

'You were in a corner scowling with a little notebook,' she told me the other day. 'I didn't dare to speak to you. You did look in my direction once and you looked straight through me. I didn't mind. I thought that I'd ask you and your wife to dinner, because I wanted to see you again. I never did. I don't know why. But your talk was wonderful. I wrote about it all in my diary. I called you Mr Ajax. You thundered and you were very funny too.'

The talk itself doesn't matter. I can only remember it very dimly, because it isn't worth remembering. The questions are always the same. Only one is worth mentioning, put to me by a large fat aggressive woman. She's asking me if the film of my first book interpreted the book faithfully.

I'm about to give my usual answer and to say something about the film, when I'm taken over by a feeling of impatience. Something is stirring inside me which I can't give a name to, unless it's simply that suddenly I'm changing, I have to be honest, there's no time to tell lies.

'I'm just not interested in the film,' I say. 'I did what I had to do contractually. I helped to publicize it and I advised on background. After that I forgot about it. It had nothing to do with me. I might have been interested if I'd written the script. But I didn't.' I sit down.

She's not satisfied. 'But it's your book. Your characters. Don't you care?'

'Not in the least. I only cared about the money.'

'That's very cynical!' she bursts out.

'I can't help that. I have to be honest. That's all that matters. I won't tell you lies. You wouldn't like me if I did.'

I sit down again, and the audience, to its credit, applauds me stormily. There's the vote of thanks, there's packing, there's driving away into an Indian summer afternoon, all in a waking dream. I'm not thinking of Vivien. There hasn't been a light in the sky and a huge voice on the road to Damascus. I'm still lost, still clueless, thinking about the children and being happy, thinking about Val and being unhappy and displaced. The wind and the sun are in my face and the hangover has vanished and I know my talk has gone well, but I'm still displaced. There's Lydia to think about too; I know that one can't go on indefinitely going to the theatre and the cinema and parties, dining out and lunching out and strolling in the park and snatching odd kisses. I know that I've been damaged. And yet I know, very dimly, that there'll be a change. I'm not out of the woods, but it's not as totally impossible that I should be out of them as it was before I came to Brotton Manor. It is three months before I shall see Vivien again.

Six

I take you now into a flat off Shaftesbury Avenue – not actually very far from Monkman Street – some three weeks after my visit to Brotton Manor. It's about six on a cold November evening. The room where Alan and Cynthia and I are sitting drinking the strongest and driest martinis I've ever tasted since my last visit to New York is very warm, very comfortable and, despite being crammed with a profusion of expensive objects, not in the least constricted. There's black and silver flock wallpaper, Stanley Spencer and L.S. Lowry reproductions, what looks like an original David Hockney, of two nude young men about to plunge into a swimming-pool, a hi-fi system, the largest colour TV I've ever seen and two china cabinets crammed with china. There is even a bookcase; all the books in it, like everything else in the room, are glossy new.

And yet I'm glad to be there, there's room to move, my worries – including a nasty demand from the Inland Revenue that very morning – are all behind me. Cynthia is some four years younger than me, tall and slim with tawny hair and grey eyes. I first met her at the Casterley Players when she came to work for the *Casterley Courier* back in 1950; we always got on well together, could talk about any subject under the sun, but somehow never seriously thought about going to bed together. She went to a Leeds newspaper in 1956, the year after I left Casterley, and then on to Fleet Street as a freelance. She isn't an organization person, which is one of the reasons that I like her. Alan, small, broad, stocky, with black hair and brown eyes and a curious agelessness about him, is her second husband. Alan sells things: what precisely I've never been able to find out except that they're new, shiny, and, so he assures me, value for money. But he's never tried to sell anything to me. He's been married to her for five years. There aren't any children, and she didn't have any children by her first marriage. Neither of them are children people, but this isn't something I've talked about with them.

Cynthia is from Casterley, of course, though she's long since lost her Yorkshire accent. Alan is from Hackney; but long since he's acquired a not unpleasant all-purpose mid-Atlantic accent. Neither makes any attempt to be trendy; but Alan's subdued grey check suit certainly didn't come off the peg and Cynthia's little black dress wasn't run up by a High Street seamstress. And he owns a Mercedes and she an Alfa Romeo. That's part of the comfort of being with them.

I am of course at this moment in the wrong place doing the wrong thing. I haven't learned anything from my experience at Brotton Manor. I have been drinking since I was eighteen and I haven't learned anything from that. I've had sex with many women and I haven't learned anything from that. For this isn't my first drink of the day. I've had lunch with my publisher and there's been two large gin and tonics, half a bottle of Nuits St George, and a slug of Rémy Martin. I've spent the rest of the afternoon sleeping it off in the flat, on Monkman Street, but if I'd had any sense, I'd have had sandwiches and coffee for lunch there, and then done some work until it was time to meet Lydia at Bertorelli's. It wasn't essential to meet my publisher today: next week would have done as well. But I'm still in a state of displacement, I'm still hurt. And I'm not trying to think it out, I'm not taking any action, unless sleeping in the spare room can be called action. And now I'm telling Cynthia and Alan all about it. I couldn't do a crazier thing, because of course Cynthia will pass it on. I know this, I don't even bother to swear Cynthia to secrecy. I'm full of booze and self-pity, I also think of myself as being the hell of a fellow, so I'm blurting it all out.

I'm feeling rather tearful now: I'm not drunk, having eaten grilled sardines and fillet steak and salad and profiteroles, and having had a good two hours' sleep.

'You'll not be able to put up with it,' Alan says. 'Christ, it's more than flesh and blood can bear! Godammit, that's the main compensation of marriage.'

'It was with ours. That, and the children. She never was much for the social life. We stopped going out together long ago.'

'That's when the trouble starts,' Cynthia says. 'Wouldn't suit you anyway, Tim. I know you, you're all for a bit of company. God, we used to have some times in the old days!'

'What, in Casterley?' Alan says. He takes my glass from me and refills it from the thermos jug. It's a big glass, nearly tumbler size.

'You've no idea, darling, no idea,' Cynthia says. 'There was a gang of us, we were up to all sorts of mad tricks. We did just what the hell we wanted when we were young. You just kept your big mouth shut about it, that's all. Funny thing, it was a very Noncomformist town. The Nonconformists were the worst of the lot. And Shirley – ' She stops suddenly.

'I don't mind,' I say. 'I knew what she was like. It's a long time ago, anyway.'

I look at the fishes in the illuminated tank. I wonder if fishes in a tank feel as one always supposes beasts in a cage feel. I like the room because it's so prosperous and comfortable and essentially cheerful, but I decide that I no more like fishes in tanks than birds or beasts in cages. I like Cynthia – we've been friends for a long time, we're a habit with each other, and I've naturally included Alan in the friendship – but now I see their faces as flesh only. It isn't just that I don't like living things being used as interior decoration, but that the room's too prosperous, too pleased

111

with itself.

'You really should try to straighten your wife out,' Cynthia says.

'Easier said than done,' I say. 'I've done my best.'

'I don't know how you stand it,' Alan says.

Through the haze of gin I think, how do I stand it? The answer is the children. As long as they're there, I never feel totally alone, I never feel totally lost. The house is happy when the children are there; and I feel that in some way I'm betraying them. I look at my watch. There's no hurry: there's no distance to go. But something has gone wrong. *I shouldn't be living like this*: I have a vision of the moors above Casterley and for no good reason I remember Gillian. She was old enough to be my mother, and it wasn't ever going to come to anything, but that was right and this is wrong. This is a moment when it's all clear, when I know that I'll pay for using alcohol as a crutch instead of a way of enhancing happiness, a grace-note, when I know that I'll pay for using another human for revenge. And then I'm pleased with myself again and sorry for myself at the same time and telling Cynthia and Alan that I'm going to give a talk at Birmingham, wink, wink, but won't actually be going very far from there, and that I've a damned good mind to tell Val where I really have been tomorrow. But I won't make waves. And I finish my drink and I'm walking to Bertorelli's because I need the fresh air and I'm walking very quickly, not staggering, not actually drunk, but riding, riding to a fall, along Charing Cross Road and down Tottenham Court Road in my new Burberry and my new fawn check worsted from Huntsman – incorrect for town, but never mind – and my shoes made to measure from Lobbs, so dark a brown that they're nearly black, better than all the people around me, my notecase stuffed with fivers and credit cards. I really am on a high, London belongs to me.

And then I'm in Bertorelli's and I'm settling down at a table near the window downstairs, feeling at home there, glad it hasn't changed and never will and ordering a large bottle of Pellegrino whilst waiting for Lydia because suddenly I'm tremendously thirsty and at long last commonsense has asserted itself: at fifty-two one can either drink or have sex. One can't have both. The strange thing is that I enjoy the Pellegrino's cool slightly saline fizziness, enjoy keeping my head clear, just as I enjoy the old menus with the old prices that they use and just as I enjoy being recognized by the waitresses, one of whom knew Augustus John. It's old here, it's wood and linen here; it's very clean, but it's old. Not antique; but no matter how spirited the customers, one always seems able to hear oneself speaking. And then Lydia's here in a blue see-through shirt with no bra and scarlet pants and high boots and her eyes sparkling, and this is what it's all about, this is living, and we have *moules marinière* – better at Bertorelli's than anywhere in the world – and scampi peperonata and Asti Spumante because this is an Italian restaurant and strega with the coffee and we're walking along to Shaftesbury Avenue kissing from time to time and I ought to be happy, oughtn't I?

I'd like to be able to say that I was thinking of Vivien, that she'd never been out of my mind since first I met her. But it wouldn't have been true. I think that she was there somewhere in my memory, but a long way back. And now, though I wasn't as sober as I should have been, the alcohol was wearing off. I no longer felt superior to the people around me, I wanted to get away from them, they were violent, they threatened me, they belonged to a world without love.

Thinking about it now, it's as if it were another person. Hadn't I realised how much punishment I'd taken? For before the rejection, before the time of displacement, despite the marriage being so disastrously wrong, there was always physical affection apart from sex, there was always that fundamental kindness between us, the animal warmth. And Vanessa was nine and Penelope eight: still before the time of displacement, one or the other would climb into bed between us in the small hours, less and less frequently now –

they change of their own accord without any hassle – but they'd still do it. There was the small warm soft figure between us, settling down with a little grunt of contentment, there was a feeling of protectiveness, there was a feeling of just for once not being dominated by one's conscious mind, of not being in the rat-race. I'd be a man, a real man. For being a man in one sense has nothing to do with sexual performance or toughness or physical strength. It has everything to do with kindness, with gentleness, with uncalculated affection. And now the balance had been destroyed.

And so here I am some four years ago, Lydia's arm in mine, stopping to kiss her from time to time, and really wanting not her, but rest. And now we're in the living area of the flat. I don't know what else to call it. It's a reasonable size, about the size of the bedroom, with the window looking on to Monkman Street. There's new dark blue fitted carpet, a small oak dining table, and four oak Windsor chairs. There's a tiny adjoining kitchenette. I've been using it for a year now: the last woman I had been here with was Hilary, a BBC research assistant nearly thirty years younger than myself, plump and blackhaired with rather bold eyes, something of a gold-digger and given to feeling me up in public which, flattering though it might have been, aroused a certain amount of antagonism amongst men her own age.

But that was some seven months ago; we ended the affair by mutual consent because in the end there was nothing to talk about. I think of her now briefly, but it isn't any help. For Hilary was simply a body. Fucking her was nothing to be proud of and nothing to be ashamed of either. I desired her the first time I met her in the BBC Club in Langham Place and I had her the third time I met her. That's what she expected of men who took her to the theatre and supper afterwards.

I help Lydia off with her short fun-fur topcoat and offer her a drink. I ought to feel desire, it must be nearly six months since I've had a woman. Her nipples seem very large. Her face is flushed, her eyes brighter than ever. We have the night before us. The kitchen is well-stocked, the linen clean, there's a lot of booze and cigarettes, no one knows where we are. And in Peter's case, I doubt if he cares. And I only feel the most appalling desolation. It's like that recurring nightmare I have of being pushed on the stage at the Casterley Players and not knowing one word of my part. Lydia takes Scotch on the rocks and sits down opposite me. I have Scotch on the rocks too, but I don't really want it.

'Is this your pad?' she asks. 'You didn't really make it clear.'

'It's owner is in California,' I say. 'He doesn't use it very often. Raymond Brove. Film director.'

'He came to one of our parties. Rather ambivalent.'

'I suppose so. I don't think he's very much interested in sex really. I keep an eye on the place.'

She puts down her drink, comes over to me and kisses me, her hand brushing my groin.

'I think we can really be very happy together. Don't you?' Her face is now softer and younger.

I smile mechanically. 'Yes. Very happy indeed.'

She lights me a cigarette: I take it from her, but don't really want it. I don't want a cigarette, I don't want the Scotch, I don't want sex. If I want anything at all, it is to go to bed alone with a cup of tea and a good book. I've never felt like this before, though I've had times when because of drink or fatigue or worry I haven't exactly been a demon lover. But I've never before felt this complete cessation of desire: even in the wrong place at the wrong time, merely to look at any attractive woman has been urgently to want her.

'It's difficult to believe, we're in the heart of the West End,' she says.

'It's an old building. The walls are thick. This is where rich Edwardian gentlemen used to keep their mistresses.'

'Peter has a pad somewhere, but he's not letting on.' She puts down her drink, stubs out her cigarette, stands up, and takes her shirt off. Though the material is so flimsy and translucent, baring her breasts seems to make them bigger. She holds out her hands to me: I go towards her and kiss her. She's trembling violently.

Now we're in the bedroom and she's sitting on the bed and I'm pulling her boots off. Now she's naked. She has an extraordinarily full mons veneris, with only the faintest fuzz of blonde pubic hair. I kiss her: she's very dry, she smells faintly of flowers. She moves away a little, then goes on to the bed to lie on top of the coverlet, her eyes covered by her hands. There's only the bedside light on, I switch it off; there's still enough light to see her. I undress quickly, leaving my clothes in a heap on the floor. I know she's very beautiful, younger naked than when clothed. I know that I like her, I know that we have the night together, I know that we're not taking anything from anyone, but I feel a huge guilt and depression.

If by now you don't know what's wrong then – particularly if you're a man – you should know. Eros is a terrible god. Just for the hell of it, he's always driving the wrong people together. Lady Chatterley bolts with the gamekeeper and the sixty-year-old vicar bolts with the twenty-year-old choirgirl. And these days as often as not the master of the house bolts with the gamekeeper and his wife with the au pair. But however ill-matched the couple may be, even if the end of it all is a suicide pact in some cheap hotel, Eros confers a tumultuous oblivion better than any drunkenness. But men at least must abide by one rule: Eros will not be used. I was trying to use him and now he was having his revenge.

I move on to the bed with her and kiss her and kiss her breasts. Her skin is soft and smooth. I put my hand between her legs, begin to explore with my fingers. If I forget about myself, give her pleasure, make her ready, then perhaps there'll be a change. And this in any case is what I've been used to doing since the age of fifteen, since the days before the pill, when heavy petting was the culmination of lovemaking and not its overture. But she pushes my hand away gently.

'No, darling, that's not for me. I just like it without any trimmings.'

There's nothing to say to that, no point in being resentful about it, no point in arguing about it, but I know that it's the end. She kisses my mouth, my chest, my belly, takes me into her mouth. I lie as if dead.

And that's enough. There's a long night and a few snatches of sleep and I'm shivering with the cold. And – this is the finishing touch – I keep having to get out of bed to go to the bathroom. It's probably because of all that I've drunk, the cold, and my nervousness. There has never been a worse night in my life, and I'm including nights on active service in Normandy when I didn't know whether I'd see the morning and nights when I've been ill and didn't even care whether I saw the morning.

At eight o'clock I awake to find her sleeping beside me. I have a slight headache. I know exactly where I am and whom I'm with. I consider for a moment beginning all over again but, already, asleep though she is, she has put herself at a distance from me. I know that nothing sexual can ever happen between us. I bathe and shave and dress and go into the kitchenette to make tea. I'm assembled now and in working order. I even feel a certain cheerfulness as I always do at this time of day. Even if yesterday was awful, there's a chance that today will be better. Strangely enough, I don't blame the flat for what has happened. I still feel that the flat's the right place for me. I don't think that Lydia's the wrong person. I'm half-afraid to speak to her, but when I bring the tea in, she smiles at me. She's wearing a light but completely opaque dressing-gown.

'That's nice.' She sips it and lights a cigarette. 'Never mind, Tim.'

'I'm sorry. I'm not like that normally. Perhaps I drank too much – '

'No. It's just that – well, your wife's won hands down without even trying. Happens all the time. Maybe you're a better Catholic than you think.'

'You're amazingly tolerant.' I reflect that it's just as well that I've never presented myself to her as the great lover, have in fact implied that I've only had the use of this flat for a month or so.

'Just reasonably civilized. It's a pity: we could have had something going. Peter's been getting rather tiresome lately.'

'You didn't tell me.'

'No. Perhaps that's the trouble. You haven't told me much either.'

'Everything gets to be too damned much. The nice thing about you is that there's nothing messy about you. All these revelations – it wouldn't be you. I've never had an unhappy moment with you.'

'Perhaps it would have been better if you had,' she says with a trace of bitterness. 'One can be too bloody civilized.'

'It's a fault on the right side. Would you like some breakfast?'

'Just toast. I'll take a bath now.'

At breakfast she's wearing a blue check shirt, an opaque one, and black slacks with her boots; I offer to phone her a taxi, but she says she has things to do in London. Alone, I wash up the breakfast things, and change the sheets. I make myself another pot of tea and go to the living area with it. This is another turning-point in my life. My body has let me down. I look out of the window and notice for the first time that there's an absurd little ornamental balcony. It's a grey dull Thursday morning; the few passers-by on Monkman Street look neither to the right nor to the left, their faces carefully neutral. I turn away: *nada*, nothing. I'm here in a flat to all intents and purposes my own, I'm not due home till ten o'clock, I have £60 in my notecase and four paid-up credit cards and two clubs and friends I can phone, and there are pubs in Fleet Street where I can always find company. This is what I dreamed of once back in Casterley teaching at Kitchener Road. And none of it means anything. I don't want to stay here and there's nowhere I want to go to. And there isn't anything I want to do. So I do the very worst thing I can do. I go to the drinks table and pour myself a stiff gin, go very slowly into the kitchenette, get ice and a bottle of tonic from the fridge, and sit down and sip slowly until twelve noon. Remember what I've said before: the only good reason for drinking is that one should be happy. It's not an anaesthetic. When things are bad it makes everything worse.

Now I'm in the street in Soho, how precisely I don't know. I'm not staggering or muttering: I'm a large man with a large capacity. But of course I'm not myself. I'm a big spoiled baby who can't get what he wants. And now I'm in a strip-club, quite near the front. There's a smell of old sweat and dust and disinfectant spray and cigarette smoke. The stage is tiny and there's a bar to the right side of it. The audience is all male, very quiet and serious, all well-dressed, all their raincoats clean. A lot of them are young.

There's a naked girl writhing on a divan with a life-sized black dummy with a ten-inch phallus. She does everything but actually put it inside herself. There isn't much happening to me yet, but as I glance at the audience, the writer inside me comes alive. These are heterosexuals, I think, who, despite all that women do to them, adore the female sex. Here they are, worshipping at the shrine. If they had affairs, if they used whores, they wouldn't be here. All they want to do is to sit quietly and look at naked women. They could, after all, be doing worse.

There's a sketch involving two young men in leopard-skins, and a girl, the main point is that they mustn't start without her. There's a sketch involving two girls in school uniforms and a young man in glasses and a mortar-board and gown. There's rather inept dancing and miming to pop records. In the end the girls are naked with their legs apart: that's what we've all come here for. I have a slight headache but the drink's beginning to wear off; I feel breathless and I know that Eros – down-at-heel, with missing teeth, not quite sober and not quite clean – is somewhere around.

The girls are quite attractive, though two at least look rather tired. They're all young with firm breasts which silicone hasn't been near. They are each in fact the girl next door; one has met girls like them, they are accessible. I'm quite happy to be where I am, I'm getting all that I want from women, there's not going to be any relationship and I don't want any relationship: all that I want is to restore the damage last night did to me, to be a man again. And I'm not a *voyeur*: the girls know I'm watching them, are indeed enjoying being watched.

And now there's a blonde on stage with a flat bold face and hard blue eyes. There's a not very graceful dance, there's the miming of another song, there's a striptease down to the traditional flimsy underwear and suspender belt and black stockings and then she's sitting naked, her legs wide apart and what is emanating from the audience isn't lust. It is worship. It's not Eros there, it's an even older god. Her hands are very busy, but as if with a will of their own, her lips are drawn back over her teeth, there is a revelation following a revelation and then my own revelation. It's very quick, but it leaves me dizzy and drained. And then there's no reason for me to stay.

It has cost me some effort to tell you this. It isn't because I'm prudish, but because I'm so proud of myself. It's bad enough revealing myself as having been impotent, but what happened to me in the strip club was positively adolescent. At fifty-two I should have had more dignity than to go into the damned place. I would have thought more of myself if I'd picked up a whore, even if I'd failed again. That's what a *real man* would have done. And that would have made a better story. I could have made the whore not too obviously a whore, young, robust, buxom, with a fresh skin and an open face. The stairway to her flat would have been narrow and steep, with peeling plaster and smelling of mice and urine. But inside the flat there'd be china Beatrix Potter figures and a crocheted cover for the *TV Times* and a book-case full of light romances – no sex before marriage, moonlight and roses and living happily ever after. But of course she'd have turned out to be as vicious and greedy as any other whore with a huge female wrestler as her pimp.

But in this book, at least, I won't dress up the truth. I emerge from the strip club into the twilight – *that mongrel time, neither day nor night* – and a dank, biting chill in the air. I won't say that it's one of my finest moments, and my headache is now throbbing savagely. Somewhere in the back of my mind, though, is a certain shabby cheerfulness. And I feel almost grateful towards the blonde girl – who, now I come to think of it, wasn't really a blonde. Although I'm not the man I was twenty-four hours ago – or at least thought I was – and although I doubt whether I'll be that man again, I still am a man. I thought that I was a colonel at least, and now I know that I'm no more than a private, a clueless and unheroic private. But I'm still in the Army, and I march on back to Monkman Street to have a bath and change and finish off the gin.

And now I'm in Casterley in the West Riding of Yorkshire a fortnight later, driving along the tree-lined High Street. This is the landscape of my dreams, the old market town still mostly in stone at the bottom of a huge heavily-wooded bowl with the moors beyond it. The river runs parallel with the High Street and the canal parallel with the river. It isn't the High Street I once knew with cobbled streets running off it one side down to the river. Now there's a huge black glass insurance company building and a car park and a concrete arts centre where once human beings lived, where once there was a community. And where once the Electric Palace and the Savoy stood – seats for sixpence at the Electric Palace, fourpence at the Savoy – are a supermarket and a Woolworth's. The heart has gone out of the High Street. But some of the old buildings are still there: I think that the Council intended to destroy it all, but the redevelopment bubble burst just in time. And that huge green bowl it's set in and the gently flowing river and the still canal are undisturbed. I can already see as I drive up Alexandre Road, the long steep road which leads to my father's home, that there's been some new building. But it doesn't amount to much; there's no money about in the north any more.

It's a fine day for November, with a bright sun, with a light cool breeze. The buildings at each side of Alexandre Road are all large and old and solid until about quarter of a mile up I see red brick and pebbledash where once there were green fields. I don't mind this: my father lives in a modern three-bedroomed detached house off Tilman Avenue, a long tree-lined road off Alexandre Road. Lucy, his second wife, made him buy it when they first married. She said that she was tired of old houses and wanted central heating and a parquet floor. The truth of it is – and I don't blame her – that she didn't want to live in a house which another woman had stamped with her very strong personality.

I stop the car for a moment after I've turned off Alexandre Road. The top is down, as it has been all the way from Boxley. There are trees all the way, mostly planes. Again, most of the houses are large and old and stone. This was once where the rich of Casterley lived. A few of them live there still. But one of the largest houses is divided into flats, another is a nursing home, another is a language school. My father's house stands in what was once part of the grounds of Hilton Manor, the home of the richest man in Casterley. But Hilton died in 1919, his eldest son died at the Somme in 1916, his youngest son went to Capri under a cloud in 1920; and his daughter married an American and went to live in California. The Manor is now a research centre, into what, no one in Casterley seems to know. But there's nothing melancholy about the road. It's a broad road, very gently curving, quiet but with life running through it, and there's the smell of the moors, one isn't shut in.

It's the trees which make Casterley, the trees and the

fields and the moors. I wouldn't feel the same if I'd been born in the average South Yorkshire town, either in the heavy woollen area or the mining and chemical and steel district around Sheffield. Casterley is for me the magic place, the perfect place to live in. Nowhere else is home. I've lived in Boxley for over twenty years, and see no reason to leave it, but it'll never be home. I have used it as I have used everything, but in the end it's Casterley which matters. For Casterley was there, even if only as a cluster of huts in the forest, when the Romans were there; Casterley was a market town back in the fourteenth century. And yet I can never live there again, and a week's the longest I can stay there. It's because of Shirley, it's because of being betrayed. It isn't Casterley's fault: I know as I look along Tilman Avenue that Casterley wishes me well. And I know that when I walk around Casterley I'll be among friends, that every other person is someone I know. I can't be lonely in Casterley.

It's turned cold suddenly and I start the car again and go round the bend to my father's house and park the car outside. I notice that his black Morris Minor convertible, twenty years old and as good as new, is parked in the drive. The house is in red brick with a grey tiled roof and a bay window on the ground floor; the white paintwork is glittering, the front lawn is sleek and moss-free, the white front door has a stained-glass window and a stained-glass fanlight. I think that my father paid about £2,500 for it in 1957; it would, like the Morris Minor, be worth much more than he paid for it now. He'd always hankered after a detached house, although I know that it had been difficult for him to leave his old home at Parker Terrace where he'd lived for twenty years. But my stepmother Lucy has always known how to manage him; better in a way than my mother had. He bought this house because she'd impressed upon him how much he'd like it, not how much she disliked the idea of living at Parker Terrace.

And now I'm inside in what my father calls the living-room at the front of the house. There's a smaller room – the study – on the other side of the hall and a dining-room adjoining. The kitchen's at the back of the house. It's very warm in the living-room, with a large new gas fire full on. It's a neat and tidy room with a three-piece suite in bright red and green loose covers, a TV in an oak reproduction Jacobean cabinet, a profusion of coffee tables, a profusion of ornaments, a profusion of framed photographs – though none of my mother and none of Lucy's first husband – and a large radiogram. And there is of course a parquet floor. It's very comfortable; it puts its best foot forward, it takes a proper pride in itself, it's a good room with no rubbish in it, everything in it was paid for in cash, it's middle-class and no mistake about it, but it's not particularly trying to impress the visitor. It's comfortable, it's friendly, there have been no screaming-matches and freak-outs here, it's marvellously normal.

We're drinking strong tea – strong but not stewed, tea with a kick in it. 'There's no tea like this in the south,' I say, as I always do.

'It's the water,' my father says, as he always does. 'Soft water. You can't have decent tea without soft water.' With a shock I realize that he's seventy-nine. He could be taken for twenty years younger; his hands are very steady with no liver spots and protruding veins, his face amazingly free from wrinkles, rosy as a baby's. He's wearing leather slippers and a fawn cardigan, but the green check shirt is newly laundered and he's wearing a tie and his dark grey slacks have a knife-edge crease. He is, in a word, regimental.

'He's well looked after,' my stepmother says. She's plump and cheerful with brown button eyes, wearing a pink angora sweater and a pleated black skirt, her legs trim in fawn. My father got rid of his Yorkshire accent as an officer in the Devonshires in the First World War; my stepmother, a teacher like him, has long since smoothed away the rough edges of her accent.

'You never get any older either,' I say. 'He must be treating you right.'

'Oh, he's not so bad once you get used to him,' she says. 'Very little trouble, is your father. Give him his books, and his baccy, and he's happy.'

'How's the history of Casterley going, father?' I ask.

He lights his pipe. It's cigarettes before noon and in the garden and a pipe after lunch. 'Oh, we're making progress. There's more material than you would think.'

We talk about that and they ask about Val and the children and I ask about my sisters and about Lucy's daughter by her first marriage, and night falls and the blinds are drawn and in amongst it all I feel a kind of envy. This is retirement. This is tranquil old age. This is a happy marriage. I'm certain of one thing about my father: he has only ever had sex with two women in the whole of his life. I have no way of knowing whether it was completely satisfying. I don't know him well enough. He is a man of the 1914 generation, for him sex is an intensely private thing. In some ways I enormously respect him. He was one of the last to go to the mills half-time and to school half-time. He filled in the gaps in his education by going to night-school, and in the end he was paid off by ending the war as a captain in the Devonshires, being given an ex-Serviceman's grant at the Casterley Teachers' Training College, and ending up as the Headmaster of Inkerman Road Primary School in Casterley. Yes, I respect him. He's no saint, but he has enormous integrity. But if I'd set out to write a history of Casterley, I would have finished it long since. He is an employee, I am a self-employed man. He's used to acting under orders, to being driven on. If he'd been ordered by anyone in authority over him to finish the history to a deadline he'd have met the deadline. But there's no one in authority over him: he'll never finish it. I wouldn't ever be as faithful a servant as him. I wouldn't ever be able to live by the rules as he does, but if I began a history of Casterley, I'd finish it. I am always discontented. He was driven on by his mother, by my mother, by Lucy. I drive myself on.

But I love him because he's so calm, so sensible, so contented, so English. There he is now with his pipe, in his cardigan and slippers, in this cosy room in this clean and tidy and well-maintained house. I'm all the better for being here and for being with him and Lucy. I'm English too, I am his son. But there's another Tim Harnforth, the wild Mick, who wants something more. I want the whole world and everything in it. Something drove my father on, or else he wouldn't have taken the night-school classes, would have ended the 1914 war as a corporal at most, would have gone into the mills like his father before him, would now have been living in a council house, would have been all his life one of the hewers of wood and drawers of water.

But he still won't finish the history of Casterley. He has cast himself in the role of retired man, he has become a pipe-smoker, he's the decent reliable man who never makes waves. And I want to make waves, I want to be a stirrer, I want everyone to know that I'm here. And now the living-room is all too cosy, everything is all too normal. And yet I'm here this weekend precisely because at my father's home there are no quarrels and freak-outs, no neuroses and no discontent. One takes refuge in Casterley as one does in a Crombie greatcoat, solid and thick, defying the coldest East wind. But have my father and Lucy forgotten that if one takes the footpath from here to Casterley Moor, that it's all wild, it's all open, it's all empty, that after an hour's walk, if the weather suddenly turns nasty, there are no landmarks, no houses, no light, only a swirling mist and penetrating coldness and penetrating loneliness?

My mother wouldn't have done to my father what Val has done to me. And neither would Lucy. They would have known enough about the swirling mist and the penetrating coldness and the penetrating loneliness of celibacy to have preserved him from it. My mother lived by the rule-book. Lucy lives by the rule-book. There are things you don't do to a man. I'm thinking about all this now, I'm tempted to tell my father and Lucy just what Val has done to me, how unhappy it's made me; and I know that I won't do it. Because they won't really understand. Because all that I'd do would be to disrupt their lives. They've worked hard enough, they've done their duty, they're entitled to peace and quiet. They are reasonable people, and and though neither of them is a professing and practising Christian, they live in the world of the broken heart and the unbroken word. They wouldn't understand Val. They're fundamentally secure and Val's fundamentally insecure. It's as simple as that.

With an effort I join them again. I turn my attention towards them, I see them as persons. I haven't really been listening to them, I haven't really been talking to them.

'Your friend Roy Holbeach's is in a sad way,' my father says.

'What's up with him, then?'

'On the bottle. Has been for a bit. Hadn't you heard?'

'Not Roy. Why there's many the night he's taken me home. I've never seen Roy drunk in my life.'

'You stay around Casterley and you'll see Roy drunk now. The wonderful thing is if you ever saw him sober these days. They had to take him off the production of *The Pirates of Penzance* for the Wetherford Players. They were at sixes and sevens with him.'

'You surprise me,' I said. 'Bit late in the day for him to turn like that. He's just about my age.'

'His wife's heartbroken,' my stepmother says. 'Can't do a thing with him. They tried to dry him out once at that place in Burley-in-Wharfedale. Comes back full of good resolutions and as bad as ever within three days.'

'His business is going to pot,' my father says. 'You make a living selling stuff cheaper than anyone else, you've got to be on your toes. Can't leave it to other people.'

'I can imagine,' I say, a trifle drily. 'It all depends upon personal contacts.'

'He doesn't keep his appointments half the time,' my father says. 'Has to leave it to others, and of course they're robbed blind.'

Roy had always been the golden boy of Casterley, coming there at twenty-three to take a routine job in the treasurer's department, making a name for himself with the Casterley Players, in fact being a founder member of the Casterley Players, borrowing money, God knows how, to set up a small shop selling kitchen equipment, crockery, household goods, dolls and vaguely improving toys, all cheaper than anywhere else and yet all indefinably trendy conversation pieces, setting up branches in Wetherford and Bingley and Ilkley, having a split level home built for him near Alexandre Park, moving upwards from a Ford Popular to a Jaguar V12 for himself and an MG Midget for his wife, president of the Casterley Civic Society, life and soul of every party. He had come to Casterley from Barnsley, he was an offcumdun, an outsider, but he was thought of from the first as being part of Casterley, he loved it as I did, and in return Casterley loved him.

'Just as well he has no children,' my stepmother says.

'Don't ask me about that,' I say. 'In some ways Ray has always been a mystery to me.'

'Mandy was getting on when they were married,' my stepmother says. She's beginning to enjoy herself and so am I. 'Always thought she was a born old maid, that one. Bit too prim, bit too neat – you know. Her father and mother courted long enough. Her mother was forty when Mandy was born.'

'Well, Roy sowed his wild oats before he settled down,' I say. 'Married or unmarried, it was all the same to Roy.'

My father seems a little restive. He's not really a gossip, he's too masculine in that strangely innocent World War One way, he senses the way that the conversation is going, and he's not very happy about it. 'Ah well, that's what young men are like,' he says.

'Roy was different,' my stepmother says. 'I was a bit surprised when he did get wed. You know what I mean?' She grins at me and, despite the grey hair, looks suddenly very young.

'I do know,' I say. Later I'll tell her what I do know and what she suspects and what everyone in Casterley suspects and if I amuse her enough, if I express myself well enough, she'll tell me the latest Casterley scandal, I'll remember it and save it up. This is one of the pleasures of staying in Casterley. But it's more than a pleasure. It's what I need. There's a community here and I have my finger on it, I am the giant Asmodeus, and I lift the roof off each house to see what is going on inside. My stepmother is of much more help to me than my father in this respect. He's not really a scandalmonger, he's not really a gossip. If ever he talks about anybody, he only talks about what is common knowledge. Whenever he has inside knowledge, it's difficult to get it out of him. He's all too honourable, all too decent, all too much a creature of the rule-book. My stepmother, once relaxed, once given the assurance of a quid pro quo, will, eyes gleaming, tell me all, professing to be deeply shocked, but enjoying herself enormously, always enraptured at the unexpectedness of human nature.

Later in the White Heifer at the bottom of the town hard by the Parish Church I bring up the subject with Chris Bandon. The White Heifer hasn't changed much since I first went there at the age of eighteen: oak panels, oak beams, white walls, old prints of old Casterley, low ceilings, stone floors: we're in a little booth with red leather cushioned seats in the bar parlour, a small room, off the main bar. It's very quiet for a Friday night. Again I am at home. Nothing bad or violent will happen to me at the White Heifer and even if I hadn't gone in with Chris, with whom I went to primary school nearly fifty years ago, I wouldn't have been lonely. And there are mullioned windows and the sound of the traffic and the sound of the river, I'm in the flow of time and I'm in the flow of the river. Chris is my age and my height, but leaner and with smaller bones, his hair entirely grey above blunt Irish features. He's almost a stage Irishman with a long upper lip and snub nose and an indefinable jauntiness. He's wearing a bright blue Irish tweed suit with a large maroon check and dark brown shoes with tassels and a maroon spotted silk tie and fawn silk shirt: he contrives to look distinguished, whereas in the same outfit I'd look like a successful bookie or a Mafia hit man. I'm wearing a maroon cashmere sweater and the fawn cashmere jacket I wore at Brotton Hall and am aware that compared with him and bearing in mind the gold bracelet watch and gold identity bracelet I look too much the media man. And then I pull myself together. It doesn't matter. I'm here in a place I love with a friend I love and the pressure is off. My personal life is a mess, but I have at least two good hours ahead of me and I'll go home tonight to people who love me.

'What's this I hear about Roy Holbeach?'

Chris grimaces. 'Pathetic. You meet him at ten in the morning smelling of whisky.'

'What's happened?'

'God knows. Nothing wrong with the business as far as I know.'

'Mandy acting up?'

'Not her.' He drains his pint and rings the bell.

'Personally, I like Roy. There was a time in my life when he was very good to me. A real friend. And I've had some damned good times with Roy. But there's something odd there.' I lower my voice. 'I've known some of his girl friends – '

'Yes, you have. Known them very well.'

'Remember Milly from the town hall? And she's just one. She told me he never made it. Everything else but. Very inventive. Of course those days one didn't have the pill. Or abortions on demand.'

'We got along very nicely.'

'I know, Chris. But Roy stopped at the point where we began.'

'He's a stupid bugger. Christ, what's he to complain of? What you've never had you never miss. He hadn't a care or responsibility in the world. Just him and Mandy and Mandy has a good job. He's still not worrying. Not like thee and me, lad.' He broadens his accent. 'The more we earn, the more we pay out.'

Joe the barman, small, grey and dour, enters. I point to our glasses. 'Same again, please, Joe. And get one for yourself.' He looks at me with an expression implying that he won't be taken in by all my fine talk, nods, and disappears. 'I'm not worrying,' I say. 'We've both done better than ever we expected to do.' This is another pleasure of Casterley. One can talk to people without having to impress them, one isn't always trying to get something from them, one isn't keeping up contacts, one isn't advertising oneself.

'I don't know know so much about that,' Chris says. 'What I wanted was to be editor of the *Sentinel*, not the good old reliable deputy.'

'Stupid cunt,' I say affectionately. 'You can still come to Fleet Street. Any time. How often do you want telling?'

'No, no, Tim. London's not for me.'

Joe enters with two pints and a Scotch on a tray, gives us the pints, drains the Scotch. 'My compliments, Tim.' He disappears. Joe always disappears. One never actually sees him leave.

'Christ,' I say, 'I think I saw a smile.'

'Funny little bugger. He's a peeping Tom. Did you know? Had up for it last week. In Alexandre Park. All hushed up.'

'Joe? Hardly thought of him as being human. I mean, always thought that when they closed up here they just folded him up and put him away in a cupboard until opening time.'

'That's where you're wrong. He has a pair of Zeiss binoculars and a lively interest in sex. Keeps him happy.'

'There's a lot I don't know about.'

'There always was, Tim. God, I remember warning you about Shirley. Would you be told? Not you.' He scowls at me. 'You're a bighead. Then what do you do? She runs off, and you run away from Casterley. But when you run away, what do you write about? You write about Casterley.'

'I've written about other places since.'

He shrugs. 'Write about what you like. I know you. There's something wrong.'

Suddenly the room has authority over me. Here are not only all the years I actually drank here, grew up here, met people here, felt life opening out here, but all my childhood, all the experience which has made me what I am. 'You know what's wrong Chris. It's Val.'

'I don't know her very well. Molly quite likes her. She's always been nice to us when we've stayed with you. I'm not criticizing you. Or her.'

'Perhaps you should have done. A long time ago.'

'You wouldn't have taken any notice. You didn't when you married Shirley.'

I suddenly have a picture of the pub from outside. Gravely Road is a long steep narrow winding road off the High Street. There's a joiner's to the left and a row of tall Victorian buildings. There are flats on the first and second floors. Gravely Road at the bottom crosses over an old stone bridge. At night one can see the lights from the building reflected on the water. Just over the bridge on the left is another pub, the Fisherman. Off to the left is a footpath into the woods on the right and branching off, leading to Laurel Park on the left. There's a narrow cobbled road on to which the White Heifer fronts which goes past the parish church to join the main road again. The buildings here are tall in a yellowish rough cast with small windows, oddly Mediterranean-looking. I feel that I'm on the verge of understanding something, simply because what exists outside is as I see it in my mind's eye inside. This is instantaneous, here and gone in a second.

'Have you been playing out, then?' Chris asks me.

'I wish it were as simple as that.' For a moment I'm tempted not to tell Chris, but I've told Cynthia and it'll be all round Casterley by now. It'll be hurtful to him if he's the last to know. I tell him the facts about Val's rejection of me,

132

but not about my fiasco with Lydia.

He's silent for a moment, then sighs. 'Christ! You do pick 'em!'

'The question is what do I do?'

'Nothing else for it. Leave her. She'll soon be on her hands and knees, begging you to come back.'

'She won't change her mind, though.'

'You'll have to have a separation then.'

'Yes. Access to the children. I'll see them alternate Saturdays, with luck. I won't get custody – ' I break off as a middle-aged couple enters the room: it's Shirley, my first wife, and Jack, her second husband. They come straight over to me. There are kisses and handshakes, it's all very civilized. Shirley, I calculate, must be like Jack nearly fifty. She's worn better than him, only slightly plump in an expensive grey worsted two-piece, her hair still warm-coloured. She has a tan in November, a smooth golden tan to accentuate her startlingly blue eyes and open, happy face. She looks too wholesome to be true, just as her diamond ring looks to big to be real. Jack has not worn so well, I'm maliciously happy to note: his hair is grey and thinning, the large bony cowboy's face is a bit too much on edge, the grey eyes a bit too watchful.

'You're looking very well, Tim,' he says. 'How the hell do you do it? And hardly a grey hair.'

'A quiet life and no business lunches.'

'Business lunches? I should be so lucky. The bottom's dropped out of textiles.'

'It always has,' I say. 'Wetherford's full of Mercedes and BMWs and Rolls and Lotuses and Jags just the same.'

'Oh God, don't encourage him to talk business,' Shirley says.

She's still a very attractive woman, but she has no power over me any longer. It's difficult to believe that once she and Jack destroyed my pride, that his stealing her from me drove me from Casterley. No, they didn't destroy my pride. They damaged it; it restored itself.

'Not talk business?' Jack says. 'You take the money from it just the same.' A bony hand squeezes her knee; she accepts it placidly. And then envy assails me. Jack won't sleep alone. I don't want to sleep with Shirley; it was all too long ago to make any difference to me now. I can see her and Jack now without hatred, but I don't desire her. I simply envy Jack the fact that his wife sleeps with him.

'What are you doing now, Tim?' Shirley asks.

'I've just finished a novel. Probably I'll be doing something for TV soon.'

'Set in the north?' She giggles. 'Shoot it in period and show the viewers what it was like when we were kids.'

'Don't worry,' I said. 'I'll use it. I use everything. I never waste a thing.'

But at that moment, for the first time in my life, I don't mean that I use everything. It hurts too much.

Seven

It's an unseasonably warm evening towards the end of January nearly four years ago. I'm in the bar of the World Writers' premises in Chelsea, a glass of lager in my hand. It's a long narrow lofty room with plain white walls and signed photographs of John O'Hara and William Sarazan and Sinclair Lewis and Bert Brecht and John Dos Passos and Elmer Rice and André Maurois and H. G. Wells and Arnold Bennett interspersed with framed cartoons, all from an era when writers were actually public personages. On the right there's a french window giving a view of a patio with a rockery and garden chairs and tables, where one can sit out in the summer. I'm sitting in one of the red plastic banquettes with Tibor and Ruth Bachony, struggling with a curious feeling of unreality. I'm not sure that I want to be there, but I can't think of anywhere else I urgently want to be.

'I remember when you signed that Vietnam letter,' Ruth is saying.

'God, do I not! Funny to think of it now. All we said was that though life was hellish for the Vietnamese with the Yanks there, it'd be even more hellish when they left. Who was right?'

Tibor shrugs. 'It doesn't do you any good being right. You pointed out a fact of life – the only choice we ever have politically is between bad and worse. Your English liberal imagines that there's choice between good and bad.'

'There is sometimes,' Ruth says sharply. 'There was in

135

the last war.'

'And there was the fire-bombing of Hamburg and the Katyn Forest and Hiroshima and even worse, Nagasaki. That isn't the half of it. No, no, my dear Ruth. Always it's the choice between bad and worse.'

'I wouldn't argue about it,' I say. 'I don't argue any more. I'm always proved wrong. I keep a low profile these days.'

'You didn't once,' Ruth says. 'You were always in trouble.'

'I'm only interested in a quiet life now.'

It's perfectly true: I'm too tired to care. I've had a long depressing meeting with my accountant, followed by two dry martinis at the American bar in the Savoy, and I'm beginning to wish that I'd stayed there. I feel all too sober and yet I don't wish to get drunk. And emerging from the back of my mind is an envy for Tibor which isn't very far from hatred. He and Ruth are acquainted with love. I'm not even acquainted with lust any more.

Roddy and June Glenthorn come over and join us, there's another round of drinks, the conversation flows away from me and it's quite enough for me to say a few noncommital words from time to time. I'm biting the bullet, I'm detaching myself. I may as well be here as anywhere else; there's nothing to go home for. I realize dimly that I'm simply killing time, that I'm burying my talent in a hole in the ground, that I'm showing the white flag. I don't want to die, but I find existence insupportable. There isn't any taste in anything, I've had my bad moments, moments which even now I can't bear to think about. But this is the worst, I'm going into emptiness, into darkness, into the black hole. And now I'm looking for my seat in the Oak Room — not entirely panelled in oak, but waist-high — and Vivien Canvey in a bright red pleated dress comes up to me.

I still don't know who she is. I don't know her name; it's on a slip of paper on the seat next to me, but it rings no bells. I do connect her with happiness, I don't know yet with whose happiness. And now, not very strongly at first, there's desire, uncomplicated desire. I fancy her. It's as simple as that. I don't think of Lydia, I don't worry about my potency, I'm simply suddenly cheerful. I have a foothold in the normal world, I don't say that all the unhappiness and bitterness disappear at once, but I do begin to see the possibility of once again knowing who I am, and where I'm going.

'I made them give me the seat next to you,' she says. 'Though you must promise to behave yourself better this time.'

We sit down; I'm aware of her scent – floral again, a little like jasmine – and her wonderful cleanness, aboundingly healthy. I smile at her. 'Was I really badly behaved? I can't remember.'

She laughs. 'You can't remember sitting in the one-and-ninepennies at Brotton Manor?'

'I do remember you. You smell so nice. But some of my memories are a bit confused . . .'

She lowers her voice. 'Do you know what you said to me?'

'Oh God, don't remind me. That was Hyde. He doesn't have any connection with me, I totally disown him.'

Cedric Easington, in a purple velvet jacket, a yellow shirt, lilac slacks, and blue suede shoes, comes on to the daïs with Joel Carfax, the speaker. Joel is speaking about writing for TV and films. He's a large, fat, untidy man with a large bristling grey beard and a deep, resonant voice, who always seems at the point of flying apart from sheer excess of energy. He's been married four times, always to small dumb blondes of child-bearing age and is always, not surprisingly, on the verge of bankruptcy.

Joel is soon in full spate. I only listen with one half of my mind. Desire is with me, very quiet and very steady and curiously domestic. There are the hazel eyes, the clear skin, the generous breasts, the long legs with the slender ankles; I enjoy looking at her, simply looking at her. But she is more, far more, than all her physical attributes. Her face is almost unlined, but it's her own face, it hasn't been lifted. I can see that she doesn't use much make-up and that she's not rigidly corseted. What I'm looking at is all Vivien. And her name suits her. I could have chosen no better: *anima, vagula, blandula* ... lively, dancing spirit, the body's beloved guest ... I observe this with great pleasure, but at the same time there's no desperate urgency. I wonder idly how old she is, but I honestly don't care. It has never been like this before. I want with one part of me to stake my claim, to start the relationship; with another part of me I'm quite content simply to sit with her. I don't want to use her, I haven't any thought of proving myself, I don't want to be revenged upon Val, I don't want to make up for the débâcle with Lydia. And I don't feel that I've wasted any time. I'm not wasting time now. A new life is beginning.

And this is the turning-point in my life. It's my last chance. There have been other chances to change my life, to impose a comely and cheerful pattern upon it, and I've let them all go by. Now the only woman in the world for me is here. Now at the age of fifty-two, battered and tired though I am, life will open out for me again. All my problems won't be solved instantly, there'll still be a great deal of grief ahead of me. In a story one can edit. One misses out the dreary boring bits. In real life they still have to be lived through. I'll have to go home tonight; Simon and Vanessa and Penelope will be asleep. Val and I will have nothing to say to each other, because she isn't in the least interested in where I've been or what I did. She's now begun smoking again: she'll have gone to bed when I come home and she'll be smoking noisily and reading with an expression on her face as if both reading and smoking were against her will. I'll go into the room which was once our room and the right words will be very carefully exchanged and I'll go downstairs and make some tea and take her a cup and go down again and drink tea in the kitchen. Yes, a new life is beginning now. But tonight when I return home there will be at least one moment of absolute desolation. I can't throw it in the wastepaper basket and there's no cutting-room in real life. It all has to be lived through: as my father has always been fond of saying, what can't be cured must be endured. But now Joel has finished and all the questions have been asked and I'm moving through into the bar with Vivien and I'm living in this moment, Boxley is thirty miles away.

I bring Vivien a gin and tonic and myself another lager and sit down on the banquette beside her.

'Here's to many future meetings.' I raise my glass. The occasion deserves a little ceremonial.

'I'll drink to that.' She glances at my glass. 'I thought Scotch was your drink.'

'Only when I want to get pissed.'

'Do you often want to get pissed? You don't look terribly boozy.'

'Quite a lot lately. But not when I'm working.'

'Oh, I like just one gin and tonic before lunch. I take it very slowly and then I unwind.'

'What do you write?'

'All sorts of things. Fashion, knitting, dressmaking, children's books, stories, poems – you name it. And I want to write TV scripts. That's why I came tonight. Well, partly – ' She giggles.

'Tell me why.' I take her hand.

'I knew you'd put your name down. So I was determined to see you again.'

She says this entirely without coquetry: she was simply stating a fact.

'I'm flattered,' I say. 'I'm not used to this.'

'You *are* used to it. You have the look about you of a man who's been thoroughly spoiled.'

'That's where you'd be wrong,' I say, thinking of Val with some bitterness.

'You look very young,' she says. 'It can't be because you've led a blameless life.'

'It's just one's metabolism,' I say. 'You look young too.'

'I won't see forty again. But actually I have led a pretty blameless life.'

'I promise not to shock you again.'

'You didn't shock me,' she said. 'In some ways you were very nice. I still have the poetry.' She pauses. '*Votre âme est un paysage choisi*. Her eyes moisten. 'It's very beautiful.'

Joel Carfax drifts over, a pint in his hand, sits beside Vivien and kisses her. 'Darling, you look wonderful. How are you? How's Neil?'

'I'm well. Neil's on location in Northumberland. As far as I know. Or looking for locations.'

'Sooner him than me in January.' He looks at me, then back at Vivien. 'Working hard, Tim?'

'Albion's nibbling. The Head of Drama's changed, and the new man isn't sure what to do with me.'

'I know, I know. New brooms sweep clean. Get rid of your predecessor's choices. Never mind if they get top ratings. You didn't choose them, so they must be lousy.'

'That's the way it goes,' I say. 'But no one made us write for TV.'

'I wish you'd write more novels,' Vivien says to me. 'You said once that you'd never write for TV. You said you were a novelist or nothing.'

'When did I say that?'

'On the radio. I've listened to you since – oh, since 1959.'

'That was when there was a living in novels.'

'I've often got angry at you on radio and TV. You're so reactionary.'

In ITV they only care about the ratings. They do something trendy now and again so that they can say they're being cultural when their franchises come up for renewals. But no ratings, no ITV, I survive because of the law of the market.'

'You survive because you're a marvellous writer,' she says. 'I like what you write for TV but I almost wish you wouldn't. You're a novelist really.'

'Who isn't?' Joel says. 'I've got twenty novels to my credit, love. And marvellous reviews. I was around long before Tim. Christ, would you believe it, once students wrote theses about me. They still do, in fact. But it doesn't pay the bills.'

'I still think that Tim should stick to novels,' Vivien says firmly. She looks at me steadily. 'Not that I'm telling you what to do.'

'No, of course not. But I wouldn't mind if you did. I think I'd listen. It's time I began to listen more.' And it occurs to me that for a long time I haven't been listening enough, that I've been talking too much, showing off too much.

'But people expect to hear you talk. They'd be disappointed if you didn't.'

Glenda Farnham has come up and taken Joel away; I'm quite happy to be among friends, Vivien and I smile at her and she smiles at us, but now we are enough company for each other. I know that we always will be.

'They expect to hear me talk, that's true. They want to be entertained. Then they'll go home and say I'd talk the hind leg off a donkey and they couldn't get a word in edgeways. But just stop talking with that sort of person and there's a ghastly silence. Then they go home and say what a crashing bore you were.'

'It's a rule of life,' she says. 'You can't win. I don't care. I talk all the time.'

'I promise to listen. I love your voice anyway. It's so clear and strong.'

'My husband says it's too damned strong. You know him – Neil Canvey, he's a director. Mostly for the BBC. You met him once.'

'Oh yes. Frankly a real Hampstead type.'

She smiles. 'We live in Hampstead. Just off Downshire Hill. Near St John's.' She hands me a card.

'That's a very good address.' It's right that it should be, it could have been nowhere else. It's her home, as it should have been mine; but by the time I realized that it was where I wanted to live prices there had gone out of my reach.

'It was in a dreadful state when first we bought it. Not that Neil wanted to buy it. He believes house-owning is exploitation. I bullied him into it. He's quite happy about living there now. When he is living there.'

I remember Tracy Mumble-Mumble. I'm not going to tell her and I'm not happy at what obviously can't make her happy, but I'm not displeased about what, not bothering with much finesse, she's telling me.

'I expect he has to travel a lot.'

'He's with his girlfriend a lot. She's nearly thirty years younger than him. An actress.'

'I'm sorry. It can't be very pleasant for you.'

'It doesn't matter.' She gives me another disconcertingly steady look. 'I wouldn't like you to have any illusions about me. Not if we are to be friends.' She grins. 'I really am a Hampstead lefty, you know. A lifelong socialist. Used to be a communist.' She grinned. 'Does that shock you?'

'Not particularly. I always tell my children when there's a socialist on TV: Children, that is a socialist, diseased in body and diseased in mind, decadent intellectually and decadent morally – unless your Daddy likes them personally, that is.'

'That's all right,' she said cheerfully. 'I feel the same way about Tories.'

'I'll tell you the truth. I don't really care. A tiny minority runs culture in this country, and they don't like it when one doesn't take them seriously. But I rather enjoy being the odd one out.'

She laughs. 'So does Neil. But he thinks everyone's hand is against him. He's feeling his age.'

'What is his age?'

'Two years younger than you. But he looks it, you don't.'

This rather pleased me. 'It's having young children.'

'My daughter Elspeth is twenty and my son Maurice is twenty-one. There won't be any more. I had a hysterectomy last year.'

'I wish my wife had had,' I said. Then I stopped. 'Never mind.'

'What were you going to tell me?'

'Just about everything,' I said. 'You have that effect upon me.'

I was realizing that the feeling of displacement had left me – or rather that I was beginning to experience what it was like to live without the feeling.

'You're quite different from the first time I met you,' she said. 'Wild enough, but gentler.'

'I'm sober now. I'm much nicer when I'm sober.'

'Is drink a problem for you?'

'Off and on. But I've never been in trouble with the police on account of it, and I've never been in hospital on account of it. I do my work on tea.'

She looked at her watch. 'Can I give you a lift anywhere?'

'Waterloo would be fine. Another drink?'

'No, this is enough. I'm driving. You have another if you want.'

'No, I don't need it.' I pushed away my half-full glass. 'I'd just as soon be alone with you.'

'So would I with you.' She stood up and I helped her on with her scarlet highwayman's cloak. She then picked up a bulging handbag, a briefcase, and two shopping-bags. I took the shopping-bags and the briefcase. 'Vivien, what on earth have you got there?'

'Oh, I do all sorts of jobs,' she said. 'Commissioned articles, books, radio scripts. And I shop.'

'I travel light myself,' I said. We went out and into a battered red Mini Estate car. I put everything except the handbag in the back, which was crammed with an assortment of dresses, dress lengths, proofs, full shopping-bags, a crate of wine, about twenty books, a bust of Julius Caesar, and a pair of gumboots. She drove very well, talking all the time.

'Don't you ever bring your car to town?'

'I hate driving. Particularly in London. I just don't have the nerve to do it any more.'

'What kind of a car do you have?'

'I have a Bug convertible. But I'll have to get rid of it

soon. My wife uses a Ford Granada Estate car. Great beast
of a thing. She likes big cars. I don't, oddly enough.'

'But you write an awful lot about them.'

'That was when they were still a novelty to me. Before the
war in my native town that was the really big deal. Once you
had a car, you'd arrived. Now I don't give a damn. All I
really care about is getting the kids through college.'

'What about your marriage?'

'Difficult to explain. Not in very good shape, I'm afraid.'

'Mine isn't,' she said. 'One hangs on. But there's only
ever been one man in my life, properly speaking.'

'I can't say the same thing about women.'

'No. I've seen them looking at you.'

'It isn't because I'm handsome. It's just that I like
women.'

We had gone over Waterloo Bridge and were going into
the roundabout. 'Left at South African Sherry,' I said.
'*South African.*'

'You enjoy making me do that.' There's amusement in
her voice.

'Only my harmless fun. The words make your hackles
rise . . . Are you free for lunch tomorrow?'

'Yes. What time?' She pauses. 'You have to invite me.'

'One. I'll meet you at the Gay Hussar in Greek Street.'

She stopped the car. I felt suddenly wildly happy. I kissed
her quickly. 'Tomorrow.'

'The Gay Hussar at one.'

She drove off, and I walked briskly into the station. I was
in the real world again. I was a person at a fixed and know-
able point in time and space. And that is the night when this
story really begins, when I first became acquainted with
happiness.

Eight

It's a bright and clear but piercingly cold January day and I'm glad to be in the warmth of the Gay Hussar talking to Victor the proprietor. Victor's appearance is entirely Hungarian – small, dark, tough, with a certain *panache* – but his accent is entirely English; he's part of the London scene. I generally feel rather flattered that he should remember me and that he always seats me downstairs which I feel, without there being any evidence for it, is the best place to be. Michael Foot passes my table and nods briefly at me; we dined with several others after a *Spectator* party once, a long time ago, and he has classified me once and for all as literary rather than political, which is of course quite correct. I wonder dimly why he wears his emphatically unattractive lank grey hair so long; it makes the thin face strangely asexual, a male maiden lady's. Marcia Williams sweeps in, looking neither to the left or the right, radiating health and energy and purposefulness: she's an attractive woman, her face has a good bone structure, but there's something curiously unreal about her. There is something unreal about everyone in politics. They make even actors and actresses seem solid and full of integrity.

Vivien enters in a red-brown skirt and jacket and a green linen shirt; it's open at the top button and I can see how smooth her neck is. She brings in fresh air, a sense of a high wind and hills and the ripple of grass and water, a sense of freedom. And she is real. She kisses me.

'I'm sorry I'm late. The traffic was jammed solid all the

way from Rosslyn Hill.'

'It doesn't matter as long as you're here.' I take her hand. 'That outfit suits you. You've very good taste.'

'You're very smart yourself. I love your jacket.'

It's a blue Irish tweed jacket with a window-pane check in off-white and orange and I'm wearing a blue and grey check Viyella shirt and brown wool tie with it. 'Oh, we're a very smart couple. Would you like a drink?'

'A gin and tonic, please.' She glances around the room. 'It's long enough since I've been here. Oh, look!' Her eyes widen. 'That's George Melly. And there's Lord Longford!'

'Not together? That would make the mind boggle.'

'No, at separate tables.'

I order the drinks, listening to her happily. For I like having public faces around me too; it's all quite harmless, because one doesn't have to agree with the politics of the owners of the public faces. Or for that matter enjoy their music. But it adds a little sparkle to life; it can only happen in the metropolis.

'I was just thinking before you came in,' I said. 'They're all quite unreal, aren't they?'

The drinks arrive, packed with ice; I've ordered two large ones. Vivien sips hers. 'Michael Foot isn't. I see him on the Heath sometimes. Wandering in a trance.'

'He can't be all bad then. And he does actually read books. Of course you live near the Heath.'

'That's right. It's straight along Downshire Hill to the Heath.'

'I know the district. I thought of living there once. But prices are sky-high. And my wife doesn't really want to leave Boxley. Her parents live there.'

'I've always wondered why you did live there.'

'I've lived there since 1955. Got a job at the grammar school after my first marriage broke up.'

'It must have hurt.'

'That was 1954. I've got over it now.'

I order goulash and dumplings and a bottle of Burgundy;

our conversation flows on, quite relaxed. We're never at a loss for words right from the beginning; but neither are we in the least worried if we don't talk all the time. When we're not speaking, we're still in communication, still together, there's always a current between us. We enjoy the food too, a meal shared between a man and a woman is a sacrament. And this is real Hungarian goulash, a cold-weather dish, a peasant dish, but with the best meat and with the right amount of spices and paprika, and the dumplings are full of taste, smooth and rich, and yet not with the faintest trace of doughiness.

'Oh God,' she says, 'I'm enjoying this. I'm quite greedy – are you?'

'If it's very good. Otherwise I'll settle for a bacon sandwich and a mug of tea. I don't eat much lunch when I'm working.'

'Have I kept you from your work?'

I shake my head. 'I have to see my agent.'

'Another novel? I do hope it's another novel.'

'I'm not absolutely sure. There's so many things I want to do, and there's never enough time. There's a hundred things I want to do, I've saved up so much material – '

She smiles at me and takes my hand. 'Oh, you're just a boy. A complicated boy. Still a boy.'

I want to shout, to sing, to dance. I can't find any way to express my great happiness at being with her. I'm already so close to her, so much at home with her. And I'm not thinking now about sex, I'm not thinking about Val, I'm not thinking about Lydia. I'm thinking for the first time in months about the spring in Wharton Woods, a mile above the north bank of the river at Casterley.

'I'm not sure that I'm a boy. I do feel there's been some mistake. I mean I feel as if I'd suddenly been lumbered with an older body. You know I'm fifty-two?'

'It doesn't matter.'

'Sometimes I feel that I've just got used to being here. I'm just about able to find my way around, and now soon it'll be time to go. At least, that's what I feel now. It's what *you* make me feel. You've been in my mind all the time since I met you again.'

'Ah, but you forgot me. You met me and forgot me for nearly three months. I didn't forget you.'

'You were there somewhere. Look, at Casterley there's a little wood, Wharton Woods, about a mile above the town. Casterley's in the West Riding, it's a little market town in the verge of the moors. Not many people know about Wharton Woods, it's a hell of a climb to get there. And beside the main path there's a stream, which is fed by this underground spring, straight out of the rock. It's like a little grotto, overshadowed by bushes. The water's absolutely clear. It's icy cold on the hottest day. It's live water, it's the best drink I'll ever have. I haven't thought about that spring for a long time. But being with you today, I'm thinking about it.'

I see her eyes fill with tears. 'Oh, Tim, you build me up. You really build me up. I'm not used to it.'

'I was only saying what I felt. But I wouldn't tear you down. I wouldn't tear anyone down. I've had enough of people trying to do it to me.'

'You're quite kind, actually. Not soft, kind. I can't imagine you hurting anybody.'

'I have done, love. Don't make me into an angel.' I push my plate away and light a cigarette, enjoying the cigarette as I have enjoyed the goulash and dumplings and Burgundy. The waiter appears.

'Can I tempt you to have some pudding?'

'A sorbet. If you're having one.'

There's a couple of glassfuls left in the bottle; I make as if to fill her glass. She covers it with her hand. 'No, I have to drive.'

And now for the first time there's a shadow over me. It seems not so long since we had an hour and half ahead of us and now we're nearly at the coffee stage. There'll be a meeting with my TV agent, Basil Lowden, at half-past three, the ride home from Waterloo and, after supper, after the parents' evening at the girls' school, there'll be loneliness. I'll be going with Val – her parents are babysitting – and we'll be meeting other couples, some of whom are normal couples, and there'll be envy. I want to stay with Vivien. There's so much that we don't know about each other.

'You're looking sad,' she says. 'Don't be sad.'

'I don't want to leave you. But I have this appointment at half-past three, and I've got to go out this evening.'

'There'll be another time.'

'I don't know that there'll ever be enough. It's like in *Faust* – you remember? *Lente, lente, curres nocte*, slowly, slowly, horses of the night. It's from a love poem. The lover wants time to pass more slowly.'

'It's beautiful.' Her eyes are moistening again. 'Oh God, you do build me up!'

'Why should I tear you down?'

I'm honestly puzzled. I'm only just beginning to know her. Later I understood.

'It doesn't matter, honey. But I knew someone once. She was very important to me, because she was so wise. And she told me that the moment a man starts to criticize, the moment he says, Do you mind if I tell you something? You say, Yes, I do mind, goodbye.'

'She was right. But there's some relationships one can't contract out of all that easily.'

'Have you a friend? Someone you can tell anything to?'

'I used to have a lot of friends. But that was in another place. A long time ago. I think that I've been using people. And they've been using me. Oh God, I don't really know – ' I touch her hand. 'But when I'm with you I feel there's some chance of me knowing one day, there's some chance of me being not quite so muddled. You're making me come alive. I'm not displaced any longer.'

'Displaced? Oh yes. That was what my friend Eva used to say. It's the danger sign. No part of your life's where it should be.'

And yet I don't tell her the truth about Val. We have already moved a long way in a short time; perhaps I'm being over-cautious. But whilst she's interested in me, warmly interested, as I am in her, she isn't the sort to want to wring me dry of information, she doesn't want to learn every secret, she's content for me to tell her in my own good time, she respects my privacy. I feel all this as we eat our sorbets in the Gay Hussar, but I can't then find the words. And this means that I don't really know what's happening to me, except that I'm happy.

I see myself there now: there is nothing about this relationship that I would want to forget. With every other woman, there have been bad happenings, mean happenings, shabby happenings; with Vivien it's always been entirely good, perhaps because she was born knowing how to give, she was born knowing how to love. She was not born knowing how to hurt. She was not born knowing how to grab everything, she was not born even knowing how to fish for compliments. She was not born knowing how to dominate and how to terrorize. She's a better person than me.

I pick up the bill. To my surprise she says, 'We go Dutch.'

'But I invited you – ' I'm not used to this. I stared at Vivien. 'I really have plenty of money.'

'If you have three dependent children to keep and educate, you don't have plenty of money. I believe in equality. I'm not going out with you just to get a free meal. I'm going out with you because I like your company. Is that understood?'

I grin at her. 'Yes, my dear. I quite understand.'

'You don't feel that your manhood is threatened?'

'It doesn't have anything to do with my manhood. I don't mind a bit. It makes a marvellous change.'

'Of course, we won't be able to do this every time we meet. I'm having an economy drive.'

'I'm always trying to. Never mind, I don't think that money's important between you and me.' I squeeze her hand. 'It's a bit like Sam Weller and Mary. Remember? "I think the materials for comfort would be found wherever Mary was" ... For comfort read happiness.'

'Tim, you're spoiling me. You keep on saying such nice things.'

'It's not difficult. You make me feel like that.'

I do not mention love. I am too surprised by the fact that we've been talking for nearly two hours and every word has counted. We each of us listen to the other. We don't feel that there are any limitations upon what we talk about, but we don't feel that there's any obligation upon us to be brilliant either. We quite simply enjoy talking. Even with Lydia, who was a clever woman and a good writer, it could be a chore, a bit too much like a rather strenuous and complicated game. With Vivien conversing is an entirely natural activity; we're running and jumping in the sunshine.

I pay the bill and we go out into the sparkling clear afternoon. I'm wearing my sheepskin coat; it's very heavy but I don't feel the weight of it. The cold retires defeated from the sheepskin; I'm left only with the best of the day, the bright sun and invigoration, a tingling in the cheeks and refreshment in the lungs. I still haven't thought of love but only of happiness.

There is no news from my agent, only the planning of future strategy. It's of no consequence: I have the feeling for once that nothing can go wrong, that things are going my way. I go straight on to Waterloo. A train is due in five minutes but I go into the Drum buffet for a cup of tea. As railway stations go, Waterloo is a good one. The trains are generally on time, the platforms are very rarely changed, and the atmosphere is less scruffy and violent than at Victoria. There isn't any *poésie du départ* there, even though one can travel from there to the sea, but today it doesn't matter, I can supply my own poetry. Sitting with my tea I am content. Everything is slowing down, I have no plans for going to bed with Vivien. I only know that I don't want to rush things. At half-past five I look at my watch and contemplate going to the bar. If ever I find myself at Waterloo at that time I have got into the habit of drinking a couple of double Scotches to anaesthetize myself and to miss the worst of the commuter rush. But that evening instead I have another cup of tea.

Passing the familiar places – Wimbledon, Surbiton, New Haw, Byfleet, West Byfleet, Woking – I feel still uplifted. Ever since Lydia the landscape from the railway has had a quality of menace. It isn't there any more. I'm not frightened any more. I don't need those two large Scotches any more. I know that there will be problems in the future, but just then I'm happy to live in the present. I'm still in Val's power. There is still going to be that appalling frustration looking at her and finding her physically attractive then to have to acknowledge that it is no use. But now I have a friend. That in the first instance is how I look upon Vivien. It is enough that I have a friend. I feel already about her that I could depend upon her, that she won't ever knowingly hurt me. I've grown tired of being hurt.

Now I'm at the Albery Theatre with Vivien, holding hands in the stalls. This is something one isn't supposed to do, particularly when it's a serious play like *Equus*, but both of us, without saying so, need this gentle and delicate affection, this evocation of adolescence and, come to think of it, the one-and-ninepennies. I derive great pleasure from looking at the stage and putting myself in the shoes of the dramatist. As I watch, I realize how I've been limiting myself, how little I've learned from the three plays I've written and all the plays I've seen. I appreciate the play in one way, it's a real play, it brings the theatre to life. In another way I hate it, because one's sympathy is being directed into the wrong place. I save this up to tell Vivien at the interval.

'There's one question I keep asking myself,' I say. 'It hasn't been answered so far. Everyone's bothered about the boy.'

'Let me think.' She frowns. 'What about the horses?'

I'm delighted. 'That's it. You read my mind. What about the horses? OK, the boy's got problems. How sad – who doesn't have problems? But we don't all go about blinding horses.'

'You're all excited,' she says tenderly. 'It's really got you going, hasn't it? Your brain's racing away, you'd love to have reviewed it, you'd love to rewrite it – '

I kiss her on the cheek. 'I'm growing. I'm reaching out. *You make everything better.*'

You make everything better: it's April, it's bright and mild and we're walking away from Kenwood House. There is all of London below us. There aren't many people about, and no sound of traffic. Vivien's wearing a floral shirt and a long print skirt; the breeze shows the shape of her legs and breasts. She has taken my arm. Now and again we stop and kiss, very lightly, with closed mouths, as teenagers used to.

'Have you done a lot of this sort of thing before?' she asks me as I put down my Burberry for us to sit on the grass. I light a cigarette.

'What sort of thing?' There is a breeze rippling the grass. The air tastes not like wine but fresh Perrier water – cold but not chilling, fizzing, very faintly saline. There is an intoxicating feeling of space.

'Friendships with women. Married women.'

'Only with you.'

She laughs. 'Darling, that's not quite the truth.'

'You'll be the last one. I'm getting old and tired. I'm slowing down.'

'You'll never slow down. You weren't slow the first time you met me.'

I grimace. 'Oh God, don't remind me how drunk I was! Everything was on top of me.'

'I know it was.' She strokes my cheek. 'I can tell when a man's been taking heavy punishment. What was wrong?'

'It's difficult to explain. I'd just had a sharp slap in the face. Or rather a kick in the balls.'

'From your wife, I take it.'

'That's right. And nothing's changed.'

'Join the club. You know about Neil and Tracy Hildon. She's young enough to be his daughter. We both must have gone wrong somewhere.'

'It's not quite like that. I wish almost that it were. It'd be more – normal . . .'

For the first time there's a certain awkwardness between us, there's a barrier, because there's something I don't want to tell her.

'Oh, my God, she hasn't turned lesbian?'

I laugh. 'Val? Nothing could be less likely.'

'Is she cold? Has she turned frigid? Some women do.'

'She didn't used to be frigid. Christ,' I said bitterly. 'Now – ' I pause. I don't want to go on. Then I go on with a rush. 'She's shut up shop. Totally.'

'How old is she?'

'Thirty-nine. Thirteen years younger than me.'

'She's younger than me. Not that I care. Do you think she'll come round?'

'No. She's like all weak people – she's terribly obstinate. The funny thing is, there are times when I don't care. I've got used to turning myself off.'

'I just can't imagine it.'

I notice how flawless her skin is. She doesn't seem to use any make-up. And there are virtually no lines. But if she has a son of twenty-one, then she is certainly over forty. I don't care. In any case I'm tired of being a father figure. Vivien is the right age for me. It is, in fact, enormously relaxing being with someone of one's own generation. We speak the same language. We're always at ease with one another.

'I never could have imagined it,' I say. 'Sex was the one good thing about our marriage. And the children.'

It's different from telling Chris Bandon. Lifelong friend though he is, one has the feeling that he thinks I've spoiled Val, that I'm too soft with her, even that I ought to try more forceful persuasion.

'Sex was the one thing I thought Neil and I had. Not all that much affection, but plenty of sex. He's very energetic and inventive. Oddly enough, I don't think that she makes him all that happy. He says she's very neurotic.'

I put my arm around her and kiss her on the cheek. She's very warm and very firm and yet again I notice how wonderfully serene her face is. 'You make me happy. I can't imagine not being happy with you. I feel as if I've come into harbour.'

'You say that to all the girls.' Her tone is gently mocking.

'No. Not ever before. When I come to think of it, it's always been like being on the open sea before.' I look around me. 'Being with you here is part of it, just sitting on the Heath, with all that green and all that space, and London below us. It's wild and free, and yet it's civilized. There's been none but happy hours here. Coleridge must have been here. And Keats. One doesn't feel bound by the calendar.'

'And Marx,' she said. 'Don't forget Karl Marx. Your *bête noire*.' Her voice was teasing.

'He's one of my heroes. He used to bring the family here for picnics. Which of course you know. Helen Demuth carried the picnic basket. It's a funny thing, but they're always in my mind. All of them. Particularly Eleanor. She was a giver, a worker who knew how to love. A lot of good it did her . . .'

'She committed suicide, didn't she?'

'Aveling made a suicide pact with her, but didn't keep his side of the bargain. And Jenny died at thirty-nine. And Laura and her husband committed suicide. All their children died in childhood.' I find the tears coming to my eyes. 'Oh Christ, I don't mind what happens to adults, but I can't stand thinking of the death of children . . .' The tears are flowing fast now, and they are flowing fast as I write these words now in my office in Boxley, because this is my one vulnerable point, this is the one sorrow which completely overwhelms me, against which I have no defence.

Vivien rocks me in her arms. 'Oh God, what a strange man you are! Whatever shall I do with you?'

I wipe my eyes and recover myself. 'Just stay with me. It's so nice here.'

I feel as if I'm drunk, I feel the Heath expanding to take in London and London expanding to take in the world. It's a good drunkenness, the best drunkenness, there'll be no hangovers and no remorse.

The breeze is turning cold now; she shivers. 'Let's walk on.'

I help her up, and kiss her again. It is still a light kiss, the mouth closed; it only lasts a few seconds, but it's perfect. I learn about her body and she learns about mine. We walk away, the turf springy under our feet.

And now we've left the Heath and are walking up Millfield Lane, a narrow lane bordered by big houses, mostly new. It's very quiet, the lawns are all manicured, the spring flowers all present and properly arranged, the paintwork gleaming. Now and again one sees a Jaguar or a Volvo or a Mercedes outside a house or a child's go-cart or a wheelbarrow. But everything is very tidy and meticulously maintained, even more so than in Boxley. This is the year in which inflation is beginning: it won't touch Millfield Lane. This is privilege – new privilege, new money – but with no trace of swagger. It is very sure of itself, just as the Labour politicians at the Gay Hussar are very sure of themselves, and what it has it will hold.

'This is very interesting,' I say. 'Everybody here's loaded, otherwise they couldn't afford to be here. But not one of the buggers is essential. If they all die tonight, no one will miss them. But where do the poor sods live who really make things and keep everything going? In high-rise blocks in hell-holes like Tower Hamlets. Patches of waste ground and derelict houses all around them and all of London's carbon monoxide. Here they get the wind from the Heath and grass and flowers and wine for dinner...'

'You sound like a socialist,' she said, amused.

'No. Politics has nothing to do with it. It's a statement of fact.'

'Was it grim in the north when you were a boy?'

'Some parts of it were grim. But not where I lived. The town's in the bottom of a big bowl with trees and fields and the moors all round it. Wetherford was a different matter. That was pretty grim. But a damned sight nicer then than now. Lots more going on and people living in the centre. It was scruffy but alive.'

'Haven't they a race problem now?'

'Good God, no! There's no race relations industry there. Consequently there's no trouble. Wetherford's dying on its feet. I don't go there any more. Only to Casterley. That's my home town. It's been mucked about with. But it's still alive.'

'Is it in your first book?'

'That's it. Mostly. I've put bits in from other places. You can't use real places.'

'I remember your first book. And I've listened to just about every broadcast you've made.'

'Supposing we had met when we were younger?'

'Then you'd probably be going with another lady now and grumbling about that bitch Vivien.'

'I don't think so. I think that we'd have always hit it off.'

'I was very young when I married. Neil was the first man I'd ever been to bed with, believe it or not. There hasn't been anyone else. Except one little flirtation. But that doesn't really count. It was because I was hurt – I found out about that little bitch Tracy.'

'How did you find out?'

'A letter. In his study. It was open. He said that he would have told me anyway.'

'Does he want to marry her?'

'He says she doesn't. I don't believe it. I've a notion that she wants marriage. And she wants children and Neil doesn't want to be a father at his age.'

'I should think not. Christ, who'd go through that again?'

'You would,' she said, and squeezed my arm. 'You wouldn't be able to deny it to a girl. And you'd be flattered by having young children. Aren't you flattered now?'

'It doesn't do my ego any harm.'

'You have quite a big ego, Tim. And you've very wild.'

'I'm sorry. I expect I've always been a rotten sod.'

'No, you're not. But you've been spoiled a bit. You're quite kind really. I wouldn't want you to change.'

'Not much prospect of that happening now.'

'Do you get depressed?'

'Not very often. There's always something happening. I'm negotiating a TV series at the moment. It's a series about crucial moments. *Changing Points* is the title provisionally. Or *Turning-Points*.'

'I read your reviews in the *Argus*. Isn't it a chore to write something people will read every week?'

'There are worse chores. Some people have to do incredibly dull and boring jobs every day of their working lives. For not very much money. They sell their souls and get short-changed.'

'Yes, we're lucky. It's in the middle of the working week and we've decided to take the day off. Or rather, the afternoon. You don't have to go home, do you?'

'Not till late.'

That is the shape of one afternoon. There is a great deal of talk. And as much of it is about subjects outside ourselves as is about ourselves. Once I would have taken that basic situation – a man and a woman, each unhappily married, getting to know each other – and would have heightened it. Every word, every gesture would have been loaded. Indeed the man might have talked about Marx and privilege and the way the working classes live and the rest of it. But in actual fact it would all have been another way of saying that he wanted to go to bed with her.

But that would have been fiction, that would have been drama. Why I remember that afternoon, why I treasure the memory, was that quite simply I enjoyed talking to her and

I enjoyed getting to know her. God knows I like sex. And sex was there. But we were mature enough not to hurry about it. It is not, for people like us, all that difficult to get someone personable to go to bed with. If one's in or anywhere near the metropolis and even only on the fringes of the arts sex is easy enough to come by. It always was; it was there for the asking even in Casterley, a little town in the West Riding, when I was young. But that afternoon on the Heath Vivien and I only cared about getting to know one another, learning to be easy together, learning, above all, how to be kind to each other. It didn't in the least matter whether we always were of the same opinion about politics or anything else.

And now I move to Monkman Street. It's early summer, the time is afternoon. We've had lunch at Bertorelli's but, rather to her astonishment, I've drunk only Pellegrino. When we go into the flat I'm feeling just a little nervous. But it seems entirely natural that I should be here with her, the place becomes a home, particularly when I've made some tea. There is no sense of hurry, no sense of being tested; we enjoy our tea and I smoke a couple of cigarettes, and then take her into the bedroom. I draw the curtains. There's still a lot of light. I kiss her, very gently, and then undress her. She's shivering – not very much, just a little.

'You've had a good deal of practice undressing ladies,' she says.

Does the earth move? Does she say that she's never known ecstasy like this before? Not at all. I explore her at my leisure, I take my mind off myself by trying to give her pleasure; when finally I enter her she is ready. And her body is mature but still the body of a younger woman, still firm and energetic, and at the same time it doesn't matter a damn, because she isn't just a body, she is Vivien, she is an individual person. And the first time is quick and I say I'm sorry.

'No, it's fine. There's plenty of time. Lie still.'

'I really love you. It's a very odd feeling.'

'I love you. But lie still. Relax. There's all the time in the world. No one can get at us here.'

And that is where we begin. It's enough to say that it gets better and better, that we grow nearer and nearer, that we are now, and always will be, perfectly at ease with each other. We don't have to please anybody but ourselves, we're not trying to live up to standards set by anyone else, we just are quite happy in an easygoing kind of way. And I'm a man again. And best of all is lying in each other's arms afterwards – secure and loving, tangled like puppies in a basket, relaxed and warm, at one with our bodies and yet beyond our bodies and beyond ourselves and beyond time and mortality.

Nine

I'm now at the Kings and Keys pub in Fleet Street at about one o'clock on a fine June afternoon four years after meeting Vivien. It's in my mind now because it was a good afternoon. Was? Is a good afternoon. I say that because it underlines an important truth: once true love – what pleasure it gives me to use that phrase – enters one's life then happiness is at compound interest, past happiness adds to present happiness. And one doesn't of course throw the past into the incinerator like an aborted baby, one lets it grow and flourish, one lets it live. And so that afternoon is with me now.

The Kings and Keys is on the left of Fleet Street going towards Ludgate Hill, quite near the *Daily Telegraph*. It's not particularly distinguished architecturally: it's just part of the block and quite easy to pass by. It's a small pub with a long bar with a black and white formica top, maroon embossed wallpaper, pink lightshades and alcoves each end. There's a long mirror opposite the bar. It isn't as well-known as places like El Vino's or the Old Cock, but I've always felt at home there. There aren't any pictures, there aren't even any funny notices, it makes absolutely no attempt to sell itself as a character among pubs, a Fleet Street institution, but nevertheless it's part of Fleet Street, there's excitement here.

I'm talking to Alec Hemsworth, the literary editor of the *Argus* in the alcove in the Fleet Street end. Alec is a tall thin man who always wears a grey suit, a white silk shirt, a silk tie, and a silk handkerchief in his breast pocket. I don't mean that he has only one suit, but that the colour of his suits is always grey. His shoes are dark brown, obviously made to measure and, no matter how inclement the weather, are always gleaming. We can in fact take the same walk together when the weather is inclement, with my shoes as gleaming as his at the beginning, but at the end of the journey my shoes are covered in mud and squelching. His are as they were at the start of the journey. He always looks freshly shaved and has a large nose, commanding rather than beaky, and a long chin – the face of Punch fined down, and without the malevolence. He's my age: his hair is thick and grey, and has been like that ever since I first met him some twenty years ago.

'I've just been thinking,' I say to him, 'that my two great pleasures have always been words and sex. Precisely because I enjoy them both so immediately. I've had a far better life than most people.'

'I don't know about the sex,' Alec says. 'It's a great pleasure of course, but extremely expensive, what with insurances and mortgages and school fees. I worked it out once, and each act of congress so far has cost me £100. A very depressing thought. However, I'll go with you about words. What do I do for a living? Basically, I read. A lot of it's rubbish, but some of it isn't. Anyway, if there were nothing else to read, I'd read cornflake packets or old copies of the *Sporting Pink*. Yes, we do lead a very pleasant life. In the small hours I often wake up in a sweat fearing I'll be rumbled and have to return to the police court circuit for the *Barnsley Chronicle*.'

'I dream I'm taking Form One A at the Boxley Grammar School on a wet Monday morning. Dry children pong. Wet children pong even worse. And even at a grammar school back in the fifties, how stupid they could be! I'd end the day used up.'

'Don't you now?'

'I've worked until dawn sometimes on a TV script. Come to that, I've worked until dawn for the *Argus* when they wanted something in a hurry. The difference is that when I do this in my job, I'm a hero, I'm made a fuss of. And there's something to show for it. Work your guts out in the average job, and who the hell cares?'

Alec smiles and glances around him. The customers are of course mostly Fleet Street – journalists and printers. But there's also office workers from Chancery Lane.

'None of these seem to be working their guts out,' he says.

'Who can tell? They might say the same about us.'

I'm struck by a feeling of helplessness. I can make a certain number of reasonable suppositions about the other customers in the pub, but what I really need to know is exactly what each one of them does. One never has enough information, one is always making bricks without straw. I can tell the journalists: journalists wear collars and ties. They may not be clean collars and ties, but one still needs a collar and tie in England to be certain of getting a foot in anywhere. The three young men in jeans and sweat shirts next to us are printers. But what is the extremely spruce middle-aged man who came in as we were talking and joined two other middle-aged men at the bar? He's ordering large Scotches and offering cigars from a large leather case. I try to listen to what he is saying, and then a blonde girl in a white gauzy dress, of the kind I term floating, enters with two young men. They sit down near us. The dress isn't tight, but it reveals her whole body. I could see the shape of her legs as she came into the pub. As she leans forward to accept a cigarette from one of the young men, I can see the outline of her nipples. Who is she, and what is her relationship to the young men?

Alec notices where I am looking. He smiles. 'They're a different species, aren't they?'

'Who is she?'

'Something on the women's page of the *Mail*. I don't know who the chaps are.'

'What puzzles me is how they afford it,' I say.

Alec glances at his watch. It's silver with Roman

numerals, it's battered, the face is yellowing and the leather strap frayed, but it looks somehow just as expensive as my gold Rolex. 'I have to get the jigsaw puzzle together. Your piece was very good this week, by the way.'

'Nice of you to say so.' Alec is always generous with his praise, which is why I've stuck with him for six years.

Alec picked up his briefcase. He stood up. 'See you soon.' He paused. 'How's Vivien?'

'She's well, and a great joy to me.'

He put his hand on my shoulder briefly. 'Give her my love.' He smiles. 'You've changed a lot. You might even be growing up.'

'That's a lopsided compliment, you bastard,' I said, but he was already out of the door.

When he's gone, I take *Private Eye* out of my briefcase and settle down quite happily. I've had some ham sandwiches and a couple of glasses of white wine with Alec, so I don't feel hungry. Some of the books which Alec has given me that morning seem readable. So I could read that evening and all the day after and not feel guilty about it because it's work and I get paid for it. It is one of those moments in my life when there's an easing-off, when one can make-and-mend or even dance and skylark. For once I'm up to date with my work.

I empty my glass and am conscious of a young man standing beside me. He is in his late twenties, with a dark grey lightweight suit, a white silk shirt, a blue and white silk tie, and an open and ingenuous face.

'Mr Harnforth? Mr *Tim* Harnforth?'

I give him my best smile. 'None other. What can I do for you?'

He names my first book, then, to my delight, my fourth, which I like the best. 'They've meant so much to me. There's things you know about my life – well, it *is* me –'

'It does me good to hear you. Writing's a lonely job –'

He sits down absently. 'I hope you don't mind –'

'Good God, no. I love it. But what's your name?'

'Lumley. Trevor Lumley. Can I buy you a drink?' He looks at me eagerly.

'A glass of white wine.'

He seems disappointed. 'Is that all?'

'That's fine. But ask me this evening and it'll be something much stronger.'

He puts down his briefcase – a new leather one with the initials TL on in gold – and reappears quickly with the wine. I lift it towards him.

'Here's to literature.'

'To literature, Mr Harnforth. *Your* literature.'

'Do you write?'

I make up my mind that if he has a manuscript, I'll read it.

He fiddles with his tie. 'I've tried to. I'm a solicitor actually.'

'You're in the right profession. Not quite as good as being a doctor or a policeman, but still pretty good. You see people under stress, particularly if you do criminal work.'

'It's rather disillusioning, Mr Harnforth. Criminal work.'

'So much the better. You have to get rid of a lot of illusions before you become a writer.'

He smiles, showing white even teeth that weren't capped. 'Oh, I have. We do more and more criminal work these days.'

'It's an ill wind – ' I feel very old, I am a father now rather than a writer, but at the same time I draw strength from his youth and his admiration.

I hand over to auto-pilot for the next ten minutes: I've heard all his questions before. But I put my best into answering them, because there's something about his youth and eagerness which touches me. Then he looks at his watch. 'I'm afraid I have an appointment.' He shakes my hand. 'It's been a great pleasure meeting you, Mr Harnforth.'

'The pleasure is mine,' I say, and return to *Private Eye*. I sip the wine, then light a cigarette. It has been a good day so far, quiet but good, and I'm meeting Vivien for tea at Fortnum's. I can tell her about my conversation with Alec and I can try to get some sense out of the thoughts which have arisen from that conversation. And of course I'll tell her about Trevor Lumley. She'll be as pleased with that as if it had happened to her.

After a while an absolute happiness sidles into my mind. I'm not drunk or even near it, but all the rough edges are sandpapered. I feel well-disposed towards everybody in the pub – again the sort of feeling Lenin had when he listened to Beethoven. I finish the wine and get a double brandy. The brandy establishes a *rapprochment* with the wine; my stomach placidly digests the sandwiches, I think again of my TV play and decide that this is my *métier*. There is half an hour to go till closing-time; I toy with the thought of finishing my brandy and having another.

And before I met Vivien that is just what I would have done and have discovered time passing more and more quickly, the pub being replaced by a taxi, the taxi by a drinking club, the drinking club by oblivion. But I finish my brandy today without any hurry and stroll along Fleet Street in the sunlight with time to spare, feeling twenty years younger than my age.

There isn't really much to look at in Fleet Street or the Strand until you come to the Law Courts, and as I pass by all that Gothic exuberance I tell myself yet again that one day I really must go to a trial.

It's one of the few bright days that year – warm but not too oppressively so, with a certain sparkle in the air. And in that year the pound is strong and the dollar weak and the tourists have grown tired of being ripped off. So London isn't over-crowded and bad-tempered, and the girls are sauntering along in their summer dresses and the holiday season isn't far off. The country's going downhill fast and the Government has broken all its promises, but that's nothing new. It can't prevent the sun from shining or damp the sparkle in the air.

And, of course, I have Vivien with me all the way. I've never been alone since I met her. I have been lonely, I'm lonely when she's not actually physically there. But in the sense of the word which really matters, she always is there, she always is with me. Yes, she is part of me. She is herself and there's no one like her, but she's part of me.

I stroll along in the sunshine and buy a Dayville Tutti-Frutti double cone at Leicester Square and an *Evening Standard* to spread on a bench to sit upon. I don't want to read, and I don't want to think. I want to be quiet and calm and enjoy the ice-cream and the fresh air and the sunshine. Leicester Square isn't exactly a place of enchantment – cinemas, sex shops, franchise joints, the seats covered in bird-lime, the public conveniences dominating it – but there is grass, there are trees, it is tatty but cheerful, scruffy but not sinister.

Not sinister, that is, as far as I know. Today I'm not interested in the dark side of life. That's an inexact phrase, come to think of it. I mean that I have no interest in the squalid. Actually, most of the people there today seem young. They're uniformly scruffy in clothes which are both drab and garish, but they seem harmless and amiable enough. There is no danger there; but there is no vitality either.

I call in at the Swiss Centre and browse in the food shop for a while. There isn't really anything there I need, but I like the atmosphere of order and plenty and scrupulous scrubbed cleanliness. It always calms me down. Shops actually are the most important of my minor pleasures. There have been periods in my life when on impulse I'd go into the shoe department here and buy a couple of pairs of Ballys, and then go on to the Burlington Arcade and buy a pair of gold cufflinks. This is not one of those periods, but I buy a heart-shaped box of Lindt chocolates for Vivien. I go out and cross Piccadilly Circus by the subway. By the Piccadilly exit there is a young man lying on his back. He has the usual uniform of blue jeans, a tatty cotton shirt, dirty track shoes; his face is grey and he breathes stertorously. He is very thin, but he looks as if he ought not to be so thin, as if not only healthy flesh but muscle and bone had wasted away.

Two young men stand beside him. One of them wears a faint silly smile like a paper hat one's forgotten one's put on. They both have shoulder-length hair. It's of the same colour – a dusty brown – and length as the young man's on the ground. He isn't drunk. People glance at him and pass by; some don't even glance.

Yes, I'm inconsistent. I said that I wasn't interested in what I call the dark side of life. But when I look at that young man – who probably will be dead a year from now if not sooner – I'm interested. I don't think that he can be much more than twenty-two. But he is finished. He doesn't really function as a human being any longer. There'll be nothing that he really enjoys. He won't care what he eats or drinks or where he sleeps or whether he is clean or dirty and, of course, he will have gone out of business sexually a long time ago. Death will come as a friend.

I put this down, inconsistent though it may be for me to do so, because it has stayed in my mind. I can't dismiss this kind of thing as once I could. I am more and more affected by these happenings. I remember them in the small hours. Yes, I still pass by on the other side. But I'm beginning to feel that I've got some responsibility for everyone. Yes, everyone. I'm beginning to feel that I can't live just for myself.

There's something which people don't always realize about writers. We don't have any limits upon our lives. Even if we have periods during which everything blows up in our faces, a phone call or a letter can transform it all. We need only to keep our nerve and keep on working. We don't have the security of the monthly salary cheque, but we don't have any bosses either.

Writers have no prestige to lose, their only status is that of licensed jester. We don't worry about keeping up with the Joneses. We don't have to live up to our incomes, we don't have to entertain, we don't even have to worry overmuch in TV or films about who has the power, but only about whether we do the work. And all this passed through my mind as I walked down Piccadilly. I was a little late, so didn't do any window-shopping. In any case, it's a long time since I've bought anything from any shop in the West End beyond the odd packet of cigarettes or book or magazine.

At Fortnum and Mason the eighteenth-century figures are coming out to strike the hour. I look at them with pleasure and then think of how they can be used in one of my secret agent stories. I put this idea out of my mind just as quickly: it spoils my enjoyment. Fortnum and Mason, as always, gives me a feeling of being even poorer than I actually am. Looking around, eavesdropping whenever I can, I become aware of the existence of two worlds. The people here are different from the people in any other grocery store. None of them individually seems taller or better-looking than any other crowd of shoppers but collectively they are. And individually they are more self-assured. Without particularly throwing their weight about they assume that the staff is there to serve them. The working class and the petit-bourgeoisie always behave towards shop assistants – and estate agents and solicitors – as if somehow they were in authority over them.

All this I put down because it's in my mind that day. This is what Vivien has done for me. I am in control again, and my life has shape and purpose. And now I take the lift to what I call the tearooms at Fortnum and Mason, standing in a crammed lift, my eyes sternly upwards, my hands folded virtuously across my chest, trying to shrink myself so as not to be suspected of trying to feel up the County ladies. It's the only safe way: London, even at Fortnum and Mason, is full of loonies.

Vivien is there when I arrive, in a white and red print dress smiling at the proof on the table. The pastel-shaded tearooms, as usual, smell of toast and China tea and are light and airy without being bleak and draughty. I kiss Vivien.

'How are you, darling?' she asks.

'All the better for seeing you. I had a bite with Alec after I handed in my piece. He sends his love.'

'I quite like Alec,' she says. 'He's not so boozy as most of them are.'

I glance at the proof. 'You're a busy bee.'

'It's just fashion.' She folds away the proof.

The waitress, a comfortable-looking middle-aged woman, comes to us immediately without me trying to catch her eye. 'What would you like, please?'

We order Indian tea and toast and jam and cakes and happiness settles over us. We don't talk but we don't need to talk. We are happy because in an interval in our lives we've snatched an hour of leisure. We finish the toast and jam and choose *mille feuilles* from the cake trolley. They're very good, oozing cream and jam; we take them very slowly. But time goes by very quickly. I tell her about the young man I'd seen flaked out in Piccadilly Underground.

'It used not to be like that,' she said. 'When we were young, we didn't have the death-wish.'

'Be fair,' I said. 'I drank a lot of beer.'

'It's not the same.'

And now, writing this, I'm overwhelmed. The memory of the whole day overwhelms me. It was all so simple. There was choosing books at Alec's office in the *Argus*, there was sandwiches and wine with Alec, there was the encounter with Trevor Lumley, there was the walk along Fleet Street and the Strand, there was ice-cream in Leicester Square, there was the Swiss Centre, and the walk along Piccadilly to Fortnum and Mason, there was tea with Vivien. She took me to Waterloo afterwards because she had an article to finish that evening.

The quality of the happiness was the same when she wasn't with me. That's what overwhelms me. I never grow used to it. I meet her every time for the first time. Let there be no mistake about it: I would rather be with her all the time. And more and more – nothing about our love is static – she's there with me. She is there with me going home from Waterloo; and there with me at my home. She isn't an obsession, she isn't a presence, she is more and more part of me.

Ten

Yes, in my end is my beginning. And it's a happy ending, just as it was a happy beginning. We're in the bath now; the time is about six. It's not a particularly luxurious bathroom – white tiles, white bath with black sides, brown lino floor, an inadequate brown bath-mat, a heated towel-rail, a hand-shower, a washbasin and an enormous old-fashioned WC with a mahogany seat on a little daïs – a real throne – and a battered white deal wall-cupboard. But the water's always piping hot. I sit always with my back to the taps, which I do even when I'm bathing alone. Vivien sits facing me. The hot water both soothes me and fills me with a sense of well-being. This bath together is as much a part of making love as the act itself. What happens after love is as important as what happens before.

'The best thing about loving you is that nothing's every ordinary,' I say to her. 'Everything's a pleasure. Everything's as if for the first time.'

'It's like that for me. We grow closer and closer.'

'I feel such tenderness for you. I never felt like that about any woman before. I sometimes wonder if any woman ever loved me before.'

'Darling, I think that lots of women did. They'd like to now if they got the chance.

I laugh. 'What if *you* get someone else?'

'No.' She rinses off the soap: her face is glowing. 'No one else would do. If I didn't have you in my life, that would be the end.'

171

'I think if anything happened to you that would be the end for me too. I can't imagine wanting anyone else. Not after you.'

'No, darling. You'd find someone else. Or they'd find you. The news would get round that you were available.' She speaks without bitterness but with a certain sadness.

'The fact is that you're a better person than me. There haven't been many women in my life I could look up to.'

'Nonsense. I'm very ordinary. Just lucky enough to be loved by you.' She stands up and I use the hand shower on her. This is part of the ritual too. We both like our shower at the same temperature, just a degree warmer than tepid, so that there's a shock of coolness and the skin tingles. Then she uses the shower on me. And whether I'm using the shower on her or she on me, there is always for those few moments a heightening of our sense of togetherness. It's as if I had her body and she mine. And I always remember the old story: once there were neither men nor women, but the two sexes were in the same being. And then those beings were split into men and women, and ever since then the two halves wander the world seeking each other.

This is the new dimension my life has been given. I live now in a world where every moment has the cadence of poetry. This is even true when I'm not with Vivien. I have always needed books and the theatre and the cinema and looking at painting in much the same way as I need air and food and drink, but over the last four years – because we enjoy these things so much together – my taste has become sharper, my understanding deeper. Yes, I have grown, and haven't realized how much I've grown until now that I look back. I don't think that I've achieved her serenity or her integrity but at least now I know what serenity and integrity can be. I'm beginning to realize that one can't be a real human being until one lives for others as well as oneself. It's taken me a long time to discover the truth of this simple maxim, which my father and mother told me often enough. By and large they lived by this maxim, and it worked. But it

172

was too simple for me, too self-evident, too sentimental; I rejected it and was unhappy because of it, I was like someone who on a bitter cold day rejects the offer of a good thick overcoat because it's of an old-fashioned cut and unbecoming colour. Yes, I've been cold because of my foolishness, but I shan't go cold again.

There is drying ourselves with huge white towels, now, there's liberal use of cologne and talc, there's a wonderful warmth and freshness which is as much below the skin as on it; I put on my blue towelling dressing-gown and slippers and go to the bedroom to dress. That's a keen pleasure too because I have a new Italian light blue safari suit, a bright red Viyella sports shirt, and sand-coloured suede shoes. I go into the kitchenette as Vivien comes into the bedroom and take out the jug of dry martini and a tray of ice cubes from the fridge. This is part of our Thursdays too. We almost always bring sandwiches into the flat and drink tea at lunchtime. From experience we know better than to mix alcohol and love. But after love and before dinner, unless we're going somewhere where we can get real cocktails, we have our aperitifs here and drink Perrier or Pellegrino with dinner. I mix the martini in the proportion of one part vermouth to nine parts gin, and the gin is always High and Dry.

I put the ice cubes in an ice-bowl and the martini and two glasses, one large, the other smaller, on a tray and carry it into the living area and smoke a cigarette whilst waiting for Vivien. I don't pour the drinks until she comes in. That's another rule of our Thursdays. I'm quite contented waiting, there's plenty of time, I don't even need to read. I am contented simply to be alive, to sit comfortably in my armchair in the sunlit room, the sound of the traffic a dim roar outside. As always, I'm conscious that this is absolute refuge, this is absolute peace, no one knows that we're here, no one can get at us, here there is no pain, no worry, no disturbance.

Vivien comes in wearing a pink and scarlet dress, and

smelling of Chanel and cleanliness and newly-laundered linen. She's changed into the dress because we're going to the theatre. And that is another pleasure ahead.

She sits down in the chair opposite me and I pour the drinks. She takes the smaller one, because she's driving. She sips.

'Ah, that's what I call a dry martini.'

'Not quite the same as a New York dry martini, but near enough.' I feel the first mouthful warm in my stomach. I taste the gin and the vermouth and even the sharpness of the twist of lemon peel, which is not, as some people appear to think, merely decoration. Again, half the pleasure I feel is in realizing her pleasure.

'Did I tell you that Neil has been acting very strangely lately? He heard you on the radio talking about Rilke, and it seems to have impressed him strongly.'

'How strangely?' Neil has known about us for some three years now.

'He was rather surprised at you knowing Rilke.'

'People are. It's because I come from the West Riding.'

I take another drink of martini; I'm nowhere near drunk, but I feel as if suspended above the ground, released from weight. 'When I was younger I was chock-full of moral indignation. But I don't care so much as once I did. I don't have the energy any more. It's funny – I feel as if I've just about got used to being on this earth. I'm just beginning to find my way around, and now it's nearly time to go.'

She comes over and kisses me. 'Not for many years yet, my darling.'

'I'd like a few years with you. Just with you. But that won't be for ten years yet, until the kids have left home. I don't know that I want to wait.'

'You will, love. You won't leave those children. It would destroy you.'

I get up and begin to pace the room. 'Whatever did I do wrong to her?'

'Sit down, pet. Finish your drink.' Her voice is soothing.

'You'll live through it. We've got now, we've got each other.'

I sit down. 'Yes, we have that. It's more than I ever expected. When I come to think of it, this wouldn't do as a love story, though. In a good love story, there's got to be a quarrel and a separation. Or at least some ridiculous misunderstanding. But we've always got on a treat.'

She laughs. 'Maybe we're too normal. We prefer being happy.'

'Do you know, you're quite right. It doesn't take much to make us cheerful. We're large and ebullient and stride along merrily – some people don't like it.'

'We're not dreaming, are we?' I've never seen her face look so alive. And she's put her finger on it. We live in the real world. We don't delude ourselves, we don't think that unpleasant truths will go away if we close our eyes. We are the same sort of person and we want the same sort of life. I want to say all this but there never is time. There never is enough time. It seems easy enough to express all this, but I'm so joyful at being with her that I can't find the words. Instead I use someone else's: '*There was a time when meadow, grove, and stream, The earth, and every common sight To me did seem Apparelled in celestial light, The glory, and the freshness of a dream . . .*'

'That's beautiful. It was my mother's favourite.'

'I only tell the truth. That's how you make me feel.'

And I do tell the truth. Don't think that it's been easy. I've broken all the rules in telling this story. I had to break them all to show exactly how it is between Vivien and me. I was tempted before I began to introduce a quarrel and a separation, to plant surprises like mines throughout the narrative. But it wouldn't have been true. Vivien and I can have our differences of opinion and God knows neither of us is perfect. But we are the two halves of the same being reunited.

I never weary of my Edward's company, nor he of mine. I understand this now. I understand, late in life but not too late, what I never understood before. There is no greater happiness than the happiness a man and a woman can give each other. Age doesn't matter. Sex looks after itself as long as love is given its proper nourishment. Old age and death don't matter. Yes, people either die or they go away, either Vivien or I will be without each other in the end. But in the meantime we are here and we are happy and fulfilled in each other.

The story continues and I don't know the end. Before I started, I wasn't sure that I'd have the time. I've had the time: there remains much more to tell you. Not only about me, not only about Vivien, but about our world, about the whole complexity of things, about the whole rich and wonderful confusion of life. If I have the time I promise to give it shape and meaning. I even dare to promise to entrance you.

Life has in a way always been too much for me, I've never been able to take it all in as I was experiencing it, I've never been able to use more than a fraction of my experience. I've tried to put it all down, I've tried to show you that there is no cause for unhappiness but every reason to rejoice. *Weep, you do well to weep,* Aloysha tells the children in the graveyard. He was right: sorrow demands expression. But Vivien and I rejoice. We have had so much, we have so much. And we tell you to rejoice, too.

And now I see us as in the end of a film. We pull the camera away from the room, it grows smaller and smaller. There are two people in one small room and outside the hugeness of the city under the sky. It's daylight now, but I see the room as being lit and I see a fire in the grate and I see darkness, a cold darkness, all around outside. Never mind it being June, it's a cold dark world outside, a world of guns and bombs and knives and a million strangers. But where Vivien and I are there is always light and warmth.